LISA-BEHRENS SMITH

MULBERRY SEEDS

A NOVELLA

Stories of Youth and Innocence

*Von —
Enjoy the adventures —
Lisa-Behrens*

Mulberry Seeds: A Novella—Stories of Youth and Innocence
Copyright © 2025 by Lisa-Behrens Smith and Spoondrift Publishing.
All rights reserved.

No part of this book may be stored or reproduced in any form or by any electronic or mechanical means, except in the case of brief quotations embodied in articles or reviews, without the written permission from the publisher or author.

The characters and events in this book are fictitious. Any similarity to real people, living or dead, is coincidental and not intended by the author.

ISBN: 979-8-9923028-0-6 (Paperback)
ISBN: 979-8-9923028-1-3 (Hardback)
ISBN: 979-8-9923028-2-0 (Ebook)

Artists, illustrators, photographers, and photographic enhancement: Debra Armstrong; Gidget Thursday McCorkle; Eric Byrne, Cheshire Grin Photography, Portland, Oregon; Lisa Araujo Davis, Paper Flower Photo, Arroyo Grande, California; and Terrie England.

A Note From the Author

I wasn't born in Texas. It didn't become home until I was around two years old, but it is the place that shaped and comforted me. When I was almost nine, we had to leave.

These narratives are inspired by memories of places, events, and people from my childhood, but they are works of fiction. Businesses, places, events, and incidents are either fully imagined or are fictional representations of current memories from my early life. Any similarity to actual events is purely coincidental. All characters, their names, and their characteristics have been completely imagined, changed, or altered, and any resemblance to actual persons, living or dead, is also purely coincidental.

I have grown to love the places and people I created, along with their adventures and reflections. My hope is that you will, too.

For Valerie

Table of Contents

Chapter 1: Big Red 1

Chapter 2: Maggie 13

Chapter 3: Neighbors 21

Chapter 4: Baby Sisters 29

Chapter 5: Little 37

Chapter 6: "This is Most Certainly True" 47

Chapter 7: The Ring 53

Chapter 8: Chicken 63

Chapter 9: Helen's House of Beauty 71

Chapter 10: September 85

1

Big Red

Jolene

My baby sister, her name's Corrine. She's three years younger than me and she can bother me all day long and sometimes clean into next week. She's got hair that curls just like mine and mostly we look the same, so people say we's cut from the same cloth. We live in Texas.

On Saturday, we was playin' in our tree house. Tanya and Brenda Rae who live next door think it's their tree house 'cause the tree grows on their side, but the house part is on our side and that makes it ours no matter what they say, and last week we put a ladder under our side so we'd have one, too. It's a nice tree house 'cept for when it rains but that ain't too often. We like it at night, too, 'cause it's kinda spooky, and last week we scared my cousin Bubba clean into Sunday when we told a ghost story that had a skeleton in it, and Bubba didn't know what that was. When we told, him he just hollered and ran in to my mama like his pants was on fire. That was fun.

Anyway, we was all in the tree house pickin' boyfriends. I was losin' 'cause Tanya's older so she always gets to pick first, and she always picks Davy Jones so I don't get him. That makes me mad. Sometimes Tanya picks Paul. But mostly she picks Davy Jones and we get to bickerin' until one of us gives up. On Sunday I was losin' and didn't want to give up, so me and my baby sister Corrine, we just ignored them until Tanya and Brenda Rae, they went in their house to play.

Corrine was settin' on the edge by our ladder pickin' tree stuff off her dress and suckin' on her finger while her feet made little twirls in the air. I like it when she does that. She's quiet then, but her mind never quits and sooner than later, it twirls faster than her feet.

"We should get us on down to the gas station for a soda," was what Corrine said that started it all. Now I know we don't have money to buy a soda 'cause my daddy, he's not workin' every day so we ain't never got no money. And my mama, she don't work until at night when my daddy gets home from workin' or tryin' to, but she uses all her tips from her snack bar job to buy food and stuff, so we don't have no money for soda. Sometimes my mama gives us a dime so's we do, but not today. She already spent her money jar at the grocery.

"Corrina," –that's my pet name for my baby sister– "You know we don't have no way to get a soda, so quit whinin' and let's go run through the sprinklers." But Corrine didn't want to

Chapter 1: Big Red

do that. She said she found a dime at school and had saved it all week, and now she was wantin' to leave to get her a Big Red.

Corrine sounded like she was fixin' to cry and I didn't want to see her bawl, so I looked at the mulberry seeds on the treehouse floor.

"Then you go ask her," I shrugged.

I knew that was dumb to say 'cause Mama don't like us to go down this new road, and I knew she wasn't leavin' 'cause we already left for the grocery once 'fore she made us go play, but sometimes she lets my baby sister get spoiled.

Corrine was off just like that runnin' into the house like she had a swarm of bees after her, but I stayed behind so maybe Mama might spoil her and get us outta her hair. I came down the ladder real slow, listenin' to Mama swearin' at the lace she was sewin' on my new church dress. Then I stopped under the tree and tried to kill some time.

I was all bent over tyin' up my shoes, which are red sneakers and I like them the best 'cept there's a white spot over my big toe where the nail's tryin' to come through 'cause I've had 'em for so long, and I was tryin' to brush the dirt off 'em, too. I was bent over so long my eyes was just startin' to bug out so's I looked like a horny toad, and then Corrine come runnin' outta the house.

She run over to me with her hand in a fist and opened it to show me a shiny dime just starin' up at us, but then she shoved it at me and whispered real loud, "Quick! Hide it!" 'fore the porch door opened and Mama called me over.

Now, I didn't have no idea why I was hidin' my baby sister's dime in my pocket and I didn't know why my mama was was callin' me over, but I know it's not a good idea to stand and wonder when Mama calls 'cause she's always sayin' that when she calls me she wants to see my face and that right quick, so I tried not to look like I swallowed a frog when I went on over and smiled, "Yes, Mama?"

"You should be knowin' a whole lot better than to send your baby sister in to ask me to do somethin' you know you're not supposed to do," was what she said. I started to say somethin' but it wasn't no use when Mama was on a roll, so I stood there and took the blame for my baby sister's idea even though I didn't come up with it.

"You know I don't want you all goin' down the road alone to that highway. It's crazy out there, and there's nutty drivers all over—worse than your daddy after Sunday supper at Uncle Varn's—and who in the world wants a squished kid, anyway?"

Then she backed herself on into the porch door and looked at me all squinty-eyed and said, "Now, get on outta here and leave me to finish this dress if you want your butt covered tomorrow when you sit in the pew!" And then she slammed the screen door in my face.

I was standin' on the stoop wonderin' why in the world do I let my baby sister get me into these spots when Corrine come up from behind me and yanked my shirt so hard I liked to strangle. I was chokin' and tryin' to turn around when I heard her whisper, "Come on! Let's go 'fore she notices we're gone!"

I still don't know why I let Corrine talk me into gettin' into trouble, but I was thirsty for a Big Red, too, so I told

Chapter 1: Big Red

Corrine to back on into the Bat Cave and wait a few minutes just in case Mama was peepin' out the window.

The Bat Cave is out by the fence that's next to our garage. There's a space just wide enough to get in so's we can set and play, and we got a big honeysuckle bush on the other side that grows over the fence and falls down and covers the entrance, just like on the TV show. We don't have all that neat bat stuff inside it, but we like to play in there and make mud pies and decorate them with beer caps, and we go in there when Mama don't want to see us. Then after a while she forgets about us and we can come out and be kids again, so me and my baby sister went into the Bat Cave. We played for a while, but then Corrine reminded me about the Big Red and I felt that dime hidin' in my pocket, just itchin' to get spent.

Me and Corrine's real good at gettin' out the side gate without makin' no noise 'cause that's one of the places we get to when we want to ditch Tanya and Brenda Rae for bein' over so long they's like cousins that won't go home. It wasn't too hard just to open the latch and sneak away, and then me and Corrine was on the street headin' for the highway.

Where we live, summers are hotter than Hades on the Fourth of July and don't no one run unless the house is on fire or somethin's hurt so bad it's bleedin', so we didn't run, but we sure hurried fast 'cause we didn't want Mama to know we was gone 'fore we got the chance to get back. All that time I had one hand holdin' onto Corrine's and the other on that dime in my pocket, and we walked so fast I forgot to step careful around the mulberries on the sidewalk, which was slick as snot after bein' mushed underfoot all summer. Corrine almost fell but I caught her up 'fore she landed on her butt 'cause Mama hates to have to try to get mulberry juice outta our clothes and that'll get us into trouble for days even if we haven't done nothin' else wrong all week.

I was still mumblin' to Corrine about bein' more careful 'round the mulberries when we saw the highway. It looked like little bitty ants crawlin' along it until we got close, and then we could look under the big trucks when they passed and see the cars on the other side. That part of the highway always kinda scares me, so I didn't look at it long but just kept lookin' at the soda machine next to the door at the gas station.

That gas station been there so long that it ain't even got a paved lot, so me and Corrine had to pick our way around the dirt and parts and pieces and grease spots 'fore we even got to the door. I think Mr. Johnson's lucky he even got a soda machine with 'lectricity to cool it 'cause he sure don't have much of nothin' else, and the dirt was pretty bad with all the trucks goin' by, but I wasn't thinkin' of that. I was lookin' for the Big Red.

Big Red's just about the best soda you can get, and when we go on car trips we always take some with us 'cause all that sugar will keep me and Corrine happy for a long time. For some reason, it don't make us throw up, and once we get outta Texas we can't never find it anyway, so Mama always takes some. It's got so much strawberry sugar in it that sometimes it makes my head buzz, but if we split one, me and Corrine, it ain't so bad.

Chapter 1: Big Red

I pulled Corrine up in front of me and made her stand where I could see her while I fished that dime outta my pocket. It was so hot I liked to pass out, and I knew Mr. Johnson wouldn't let me stick my head in with the ice creams so I figured puttin' my face in next to the soda was gonna have to make do. I dropped the dime into the machine and opened up the door real careful so it wouldn't pull shut, and then I stuck my face inside. I was all squinted up lookin' like I was tryin' to read all the different kinds of soda even though I could see "Big Red" big as life on a bottle cap. Corrine looked like a fish through the sweaty glass door and I was glad I was coolin' off first when she tried to cut in, but then I pulled out a Big Red and closed the door.

"Come on," I told her while I pushed the bottle under the opener and popped off the cap. "We got to get home."

Corrine tried to stop and pick the cap outta the barrel but I reminded her it wouldn't be so good for Mama to see it if we forgot to get rid of it in the Bat Cave when we got home. By the time she quit lookin' I'd had mosta that Big Red and was takin' my time getting' across the dirt and back onto the highway.

"Gimme some!" whined Corrine. "It was my dime!"

I ignored her and had my fill 'cause Corrina's still a baby and when she drinks soda from a bottle she don't know how to let the air pass. She ends up suckin' her tongue up inside the bottle so it looks like Uncle Benny's boil, and then I lose my stomach tryin' to drink after her. I gave in and passed our soda to her. But I kept my eyes on the road and didn't look at her until she dropped the bottle on the side of the road. Then I saw I'd have to try to clean up her mouth. I liked to rub it raw where the Big Red left its stain, but it was no use so I told her to suck on her lip and make it look like she just got a sore.

I didn't pay much attention to the rest of the time goin' home. We stopped along the way to watch some ants and Corrine almost caught a lizard and I had to keep her from runnin' into the street after it. We stopped at someone's house and sat on the grass and watched the cars go by until Corrine had counted all the way up to fifty-nineteen, and then I remembered we had to get home. 'Bout the time we hit Tanya and Brenda Rae's mulberry tree, I could see Mama settin' in the front window. I just knew she was waitin' for us.

I pulled Corrine to Tanya and Brenda Rae's side yard so quick I liked to pull her arm out the socket.

"We got to hide, Corrina!" I hissed. "Mama knows we been gone 'cause she's settin' the the window, and when you see her, you got to lie!" I looked over my shoulder, then back at Corrine's quiverin' red lip. "Can you lie for me Corrina?" I asked.

My only answer was some tears my baby sister started spillin'. She forgot all about suckin' on her lower lip so I rubbed it again to cover up the soda, and then we went into Tanya and Brenda Rae's side gate and across their back yard. I was movin' pretty fast up their ladder to the tree house until I remembered Corrine behind me, but she was right there. She had stopped cryin' so I figured she was almost as scared as me. I pulled her up and over the floor and lifted her onto our ladder 'fore I followed her down, and then we hit the

Chapter 1: Big Red

ground and ran for the Bat Cave like the devil himself was on our heels.

I was breathin' pretty hard when we got into the Bat Cave and Corrine was too, so we tried to settle down by layin' on the ground and lookin' up through the honeysuckle.

"You 'spose she'll whoop us?" Corrine asked. I figured my Mama would but I didn't want to go scarin' my baby sister into tellin' the truth.

"Not if we distract her," I answered.

"How we gonna 'stract her?"

I thought for a second 'fore I jumped up and set to makin' a mud pie. I had taken Mama's flour sifter from the kitchen the week before so's I could make the dirt clods into powdered-sugar toppin' for the pies and I forgot to take it back. I hadn't found a good time since to get it back so it was still out in the Bat Cave with us. I knew it would be a good distraction so I started droppin' clods and makin' icing. I was still hard at it when I heard the porch door open and Mama callin' like we was in the next state.

I gave Corrine the pie and held onto the sifter, and then we came outta the Bat Cave lookin' pretty innocent, but Mama had Tanya and Brenda Rae's mama right behind her.

"We made you a cake, Mama," I said while I pushed Corrine up in front of me, "and I made icing with your sifter." Corrine just smiled like a idiot.

Mama's eyes went straight to the sifter, and bein' as how she was a mama and could have yanked us from across a room without ever havin' to get up, she was able to snatch it outta my hand 'fore I even knew it was missin', and then she stared at me hard and asked me where we'd gone to.

Corrine's mind musta taken a vacation to the loony-bin when she answered, "We's over at Tanya and Brenda Rae's, Mama. Honest."

'Bout that time, Tanya and Brenda Rae's mama 'scused herself and Mama didn't even show her to the door so I knew we was in for it. Mama backed in the kitchen and pitched the sifter into the sink without ever takin' her eyes offa us, and then she bent over real sweet and pulled at Corrine's shirt. Sure enough, there was the proof, all down the front of it.

"No, I don't think you were," she said, starin' at Corrine without even straightenin' up.

My mind was workin' on a different lie when Corrine cut loose with the biggest strawberry-sugar burp I ever did hear, right in Mama's face. I liked to wet my pants thinkin' of Mama's paddle board inside the porch door, and I figured we'd hear about it for a week 'fore my daddy got home and saw our little wood puppies. Mama, she got one of those little cut out dog houses and puppy dogs and a mama dog and a daddy dog, and they all hang on the kitchen wall. When we're bad, she puts our puppies in the dog house and my daddy sees 'em first thing when he walks in the kitchen for a beer, so I figured we was flat-out mud.

My mama didn't say a word when she straightened up tall and opened up the porch door for us to get inside. I figured we would get a lickin' like no other 'cause Mama always tells me I'm the oldest and got to watch out and be responsible. My butt was already smartin' just walkin' in the door.

Chapter 1: Big Red

One thing I know for sure is it ain't a good idea to talk back to Mama, but I figured I wasn't gonna get in no more trouble than I was already in so I decided to take a chance. I tried to sound real grown up when I said, "Mama," and tried to breathe in without shakin'.

"I's just tryin' to take care of Corrine and stay outta your hair like you told us," I breathed out as fast as I could. "And I know you think I'm still a baby, but I ain't no more." I tried to make it all make sense to her the way it did to me when I finished, "And it ain't like I went off and got us killed or somethin'."

And then I waited. I thought of the paddle board and the dog house and our puppies and thought of how I was really gonna get it now, but my Mama stopped movin', and just like that, she got closer to Jesus on the forgivin' side.

She never said a word but yanked us on over to the sink and washed that sticky soda-water-dirt offa our hands, and just about drowned us dunkin' our faces under the faucet, and then she sat me and Corrine down at the table and put a glass of ice in front of us. And not that kind of glass that we's used to that's little-bitty and metal, but a real glass that breaks if you drop it and big like a grown-up's, with ice stacked up so high it was bustin' out the top.

Now my mama don't like sweets in the house and she only buys one kind and that's her soda for a whole week. She buys her and my daddy two six-packs of Lone Star or Miller High Life and she buys one six-pack of her soda every week, and then she gets herself one outta the ice box every night and takes it down slow after we go to bed and her and my daddy watch TV, and then on Sunday after church she gets one beer and my daddy, he drinks the rest, but her soda lasts her all week, and she don't even offer it to company, not even my grandma and granddaddy when they come to visit all the way from California. I figured my mama's marbles musta been rollin' on the floor 'cause she opened up the ice box and pulled out a soda colder than was our Big Red at the gas station and watched us the whole time she took down the church key to pop the top. Then she walked on over to us and poured my glass full and Corrine's glass full and left herself just two or three little swallows from the bottle.

I don't rightly remember everything' Mama had to say that day 'cept she guessed we'd gone off and growed up a little while she wasn't lookin'. She made me tell her how did we get down to the gas station and where did we cross the road and did we walk close to the highway and did I hold my baby sister's hand and what did we do on the way back. Then when the soda and questions was finished, she sent us in for a bath and told us we couldn't play outside for the rest of the day, but she didn't paddle me, and when I got outta the bath, my puppy was still hangin' on the wall right next to Mama's.

The next Saturday 'fore Mama took us to the grocery, she took a dime outta her grocery jar and laid it on the window sill above the kitchen sink, and on Sunday after church and 'fore we went to supper at Aunt Odella and Uncle Varn's, she leaned down and looked at me real close when she said to hold it tight in one hand and to hold onto Corrina with the other while we walked on down to the gas station for a Big Red.

2
Maggie
Corrine

Today I get to go to the flower shop. I ain't ever been at a flower shop. Mama goes every Saturday to buy the church flowers but she don't never take me. She goes alone or with Jolene but today she gonna take only me. We gonna buy daisies. Mama say daisies are happy and the best flowers for a friend.

My best friend is Maggie. Every mornin' we go together to Miss Jackson's class in Room Number Four. Maggie got a older sister named Mary and Mary's in class with Jolene. But Jolene don't like Mary. Jolene say Mary's a pill and too much a sissy for her. Maggie ain't a pill. She likes to play rough and we play leapfrog all mornin' 'cept when we swing. I don't like to swing all the time though. Maggie's better'n me and sometimes that makes me mad.

Maggie looks kinda funny. She got a forehead that goes on for days. It starts in the right place but it ends up way up almost on the top of her head. She all the time wearin' a bandana to cover it. She holds it down with a little bitty bobby pin. Then all we see is her white, white hair.

She looks funny too 'cause she got eyes like ice and no color on her skin. Mama say she a albino. We had a pony at my Poppy's farm one time that was a albino but he had red eyes. He was born all white but his mama was white so we thought he was just like his mama. Then we saw his eyes. It was for sure the devil himself lookin' at us. Mama say it was just a pony but I don't believe it. Pastor's all the time preachin' in church on Sunday 'bout the devil. All the fire in hell burned him up so bad he turned all white hot with red in his eyes. Good thing Maggie got some blue in her eyes or she'd be the devil too. I know that. I know it for a fact.

We been friends ever since we both started first grade. Maggie's slow in math and she counts on her fingers. Sometimes when there ain't no one lookin' she puts marks on the desk with her pencil. Then she counts the marks. Sometimes she puts the marks inside circles and count's 'em all. I seen her lips movin' and I seen the marks when we clean desks at the end of the day so I know she don't do good in math. I try to help but she don't like numbers. She say it's no fun.

One thing Maggie does better'n anyone else is play rough. She can run and jump better'n any boy in our class and some of the second graders too. She say that's cause' she got a boy cousin but I got a boy cousin too. I got lotsa boy cousins but

Chapter 2: Maggie

all of them put together can't play better'n Maggie. I say I don't guess it's true but she say yes it is. She say one time she 'bout wore herself out tryin' to keep up with him chasin' after fireflies and she run straight into a cactus patch with no shoes on. 'Fore she had to decide whether to scream or keep runnin' she run clear outta the other side. She say chasin' fireflies make her happiest 'cause she don't gotta think of nothin' else. I like fireflies too but I don't think I'd run into a cactus patch for 'em.

Maggie swings best too. I like it okay but she always swings highest and if I'm tired that makes me mad. One time we was in a contest and she was highest again. That day I said you can't come to my house again ever and it made Maggie cry. She cried hard but I didn't care. I just wanted her to go away and leave me alone. I turned my back on her and played with Fred. Playin' with a boy is the worst thing to get back at someone you're mad at and especially Fred. He's the worst. He eats boogers.

Maggie ran away but she ran into Miss Jackson and told on me. We ain't supposed to hurt each other 'cause we go to a church school. Pastor and Miss Jackson's all the time screamin' on the playground Stop it! and Be nice! like they gotta scream it all the way into our heads. After Maggie done told on me Miss Jackson came over like she was on fire and talked to me 'bout bein' unkind. I didn't know I was bein' unkind. I just thought I was bein' mad. I had to 'pologize then. That happens a lot. Mama say it's 'cause I don't think how other people feel. I do think about it though. I do. I just don't care when I get mad.

Mostly though me and Maggie get along fine. We like to do art together too. We set together at art table and share things. I have the best scissors but Maggie's left-handed. She can't use my scissors. And I got that brown runny paste so we mostly use hers. She got the white paste with the dipper and when Maggie don't look me and Arlene eat it. Then Maggie wonders where did it all go. I say I don't know and give her my brown yucky paste. We share paint too. My favorite color's purple and Maggie likes blue. We don't eat the paint.

One day a long time ago Maggie didn't come to school. I waited on the steps but I didn't see her all mornin'. Then I waited on the playground and sat in the sandbox so long I got chiggers under my socks and up my skirt. I still waited for her after the bell rung but Pastor come to close the gate. I took off inside and down the hall to my desk just 'fore Miss Jackson called my name. I kept waitin' for Maggie but she didn't come in. After nap I had to do art all by myself and it wasn't no fun. I didn't have the good paste but I had paint so I painted a picture of our class with me and Maggie in front.

Maggie's mama come in that day just 'fore school was out. She say Maggie's sick. She picked up Maggie's sweater off the hook in back and some things outta her desk. She talked to Miss Jackson and they whispered a lot. She blowed her nose a lot too. I tried to ask when is Maggie comin' back. I even said 'scuse me but they say Stop interrupting! and made me go set in The Bad Chair by Miss Jackson's desk. I still couldn't hear nothin'. Then I walked home with Jolene and she say Maggie's real sick and can't come back for a while. I watched for Maggie

Chapter 2: Maggie

for forever but I didn't see her after that. I didn't know what happened to her and didn't nobody tell me after that.

It was a long time Maggie was gone. Sometimes her mama would call but Maggie didn't call. Just her mama. I asked one time what her mama say but Mama say it's nothin'. The one time she say Maggie's gonna come back soon. I asked Mama to dial the phone for me too 'cause I don't know how to call the number. I only know my phone number which is DI49153. But that number don't work for callin' Maggie but just for people callin' us. Mama didn't call her for me though. She say I don't want to bother them and they're busy like us.

Then one day Miss Jackson told us you can make whatever you want for art. I made Maggie a picture card. I said I Miss You on it and painted it blue on the outside. On the inside I put two swings with me and Maggie. I made her all white with her red bandana and her blue skirt. I made myself with blond hair and a red dress and I was swingin' higher than Maggie. I put my name Corrine on the bottom and hung it on the line to dry. Miss Jackson said I'll send it. It dried for 'bout a week 'fore she finally took it down. I watched it every day to see if she remembered 'til she took it down and then she said I'll send it.

Monday the office lady come into class and whispered to Miss Jackson and she left. The office lady stayed and after a long time Miss Jackson come back into class with Pastor. They was holdin' a card. They say this is from Maggie's mama. Maggie's gone. She got somethin' in her blood and the doctors tried real hard to get it out. They tried real hard but they couldn't get it out. So Maggie's gone. And they say don't be sad 'cause her soul went to be with Jesus in heaven. I know what they mean. They don't mean she gone somewhere. They say gone. But they mean she dead.

I don't feel happy 'bout Maggie in heaven. I don't even though they say we should. Pastor's all the time sayin' that when we go to heaven we won't feel hot or cold or hungry or tired and we can sing and be with Jesus all the time. I can't even think what that's like. And I wouldn't be happy if I didn't have Jolene and Mama and Daddy and Odella and Uncle Varn and even Bubba. The rest sounds good but not Maggie bein' alone.

They smile and say we should be happy to Jesus and then they say let's pray and we did. Then Pastor patted Miss Jackson on the shoulder and she walked him to the door. Miss Jackson picked up her book and we was s'posed to do readin'. I tried to read but all I thought about all day was Maggie bein' dead.

I know about dyin'. I do. One time Ginger had a runt that was so little it couldn't get no milk. Mama and Daddy watched it 'til all the other puppies was twice as big and stepped on it and it cried. They told me and Jolene it's sick. Then one night after me and Jolene went to bed I heard Daddy say I gotta do it. He say we can't afford no vet so I'll do it. I watched him out my window. He picked it up and put it in a towel and wrapped it up even up 'round its head. Then he put it in his arms and held it tight for a real long time. Ginger was whinin' and runnin' 'round his legs and steppin' on all her puppies but she couldn't get to her runt. Then Daddy took it out the gate and dropped it in the garbage.

Chapter 2: Maggie

Next day Daddy lied. He say the runt died and I buried it in the flowers. He ate his eggs and toast and didn't say no more. He just dipped his toast in his eggs. Then he left to help with farm chores.

Later I went to the garbage can and lifted the lid. There was the runt all tiny in the trash. I poked it but it didn't move. That's when I knowed 'bout dyin'. Didn't no one kill Maggie but she dead like that too and she ain't comin' back neither.

Later I asked Mama can I go to church and see Maggie get buried. Mama say no. She say you're too little. She say it would be sad for you to see Maggie get buried. I don't know why. I know about buryin'. I seen Daddy bury a farm cow and our birds when they die. He digs a hole and puts 'em in. He's nice and don't throw 'em. Sometimes we draw a little picture or write notes to put in. I say goodbye and prayers. Then Daddy covers 'em up and pretty soon there's grass. Daddy sometimes puts a tiny tree or some flower plants to tell me the spot where he put 'em so's I know where to find 'em. Daddy didn't bury the runt. But all them others I know where to find 'em. Sometimes I visit and talk to them.

Then today Mama come out in a black dress and her shiny heels and long gloves and say I'm goin' to the funeral. And Daddy too if he finishes with Poppy and gets home pretty soon. I wanted to go but she say you and Jolene gotta stay next door and play.

I didn't wanna go next door and I sure didn't wanna play with those babies Jackie and Joe-Joe like nothin' happened. It wasn't fair. I didn't get to tell Maggie bye and see you later and it wasn't fair that no one listened to me when I say I want to say bye to Maggie. I cried and yelled all kinds of things at Mama but she say you're upset and you go lay down. I didn't wanna lay down.

I screamed like Pastor and Miss Jackson on the playground tryin' to get my words into her head. I told Mama you ain't bein kind. You didn't call her for me. You didn't tell me 'fore she died that Maggie ain't comin' back. She ain't comin' back. I know what dead is and she ain't comin' back. I wanna say bye and prayers. I wanna see where she is so's I know where to find her.

I yelled and cried so hard I got the chee-hunks. I sat on Mama's lap and chee-hunked and she played with my hair. She rocked me and played with my hair and say I promise Corrina. I promise to take you. She say you can't go see her get buried 'cause her mama don't want no kids there but I promise to take you to put flowers so's you can find her.

That's why we gonna buy daisies. Mama say I can't plant no tree but there's a little cup for flowers. And she say I'll bring you whenever you ask. I say do you promise and she say yes. I know she means it. Jolene say sometimes Mama makes promises and then she breaks 'em. She don't mean to is what Jolene say but she can't keep all them promises.

But this one she means. I watched her when she say it and she means it. She say I promise you always gonna know where to find your Maggie.

3

Neighbors

Jolene

Corrine ain't half bad for a baby sister. She mostly remembers to pick up her toys and says 'scuse me when she burps and 'cept for the time we was at school and she tried to open a mayonnaise packet by smashin' it between her hands so's it exploded and shot Mrs. Massey on the top of her head with Helmann's, she don't embarrass me much, but every now and then Corrine gets so full of rotten that Mama only got the choice of beat her or send her to bed. One day, Corrine went to bed early and didn't even wait for Mama to tell her.

I seen Corrine do some pretty rotten things but mostly it happened with Jackie and her brother Joe-Joe. They lived next door at our old house 'fore we moved next to Tanya and Brenda Rae. Jackie was younger than Corrine, and Joe-Joe was still in diapers, and it didn't help that my mama and daddy said their mama and daddy, they was idiots. Mostly my daddy said that when their daddy got up on Saturday 'fore cartoons even started and mowed their backyard. Pretty soon my daddy, he was awake and standin' in front of the kitchen window in his underwear drinkin' a beer and laughin' out loud 'cause he said Jackie's daddy didn't know how to mow the yard right. I don't know how it can be hard. I watch my mama do it all the time. You just pull on the string and then it starts and you walk behind the mower, but he said Jackie's daddy was a idiot 'cause he got a fancy 'lectric mower and he was all the time tryin' not to run over the cord and makin' criss-crosses and circles and curly-snake patterns in the yard. My daddy thought that was funny. I thought it was funny my daddy stood in front of the window in his underwear.

Jackie wasn't so bad and she was fun to play with even though she was still little and liked to say her name "Jack-uh-lean" like the president used to about Mrs. Kennedy, but Corrine didn't like Jackie ever since she peed on our slide. That day Jackie was playin' so hard that she forgot to go back home to get her mama to help her in the bathroom. She was all the way up top of the slide when it happened. She got this look like she was scared and then her mouth turned into a giant O, and then we saw it steamin' like water off a bath. Corrine started screamin' when it ran down the sides and dripped onto the grass. She ran and got the water hose and started washin' the pee off the slide and the next thing I know she'd turned that hose on Jackie and then Jackie run away home and didn't come back. After that Corrine didn't

Chapter 3: Neighbors

want Jackie to come play 'cause she said she didn't want no pee on her outside toys but when Corrine wasn't around I let Jackie come play and she was okay. She didn't pee on nothin' else and just to make her feel better I told her about the time Corrine wet the bed. Corrine got mad and said, "No I didn't!" and lied about it like she did that time she went behind my daddy's chair and ate a whole box of Pepto Bismol, but after that Jackie felt better.

One day we was playin' outside on our driveway with our new skates. They ain't really new 'cause they came from my cousins Tammy and Rocky and Junior when they got them new fancy skates that look like boots and lace up and got a big rubber stop, big as a marshmallow just under the toe. Then we got the old ones with metal clips on the sides and a key to help adjust the size. I don't care if they're old. They still fit and they're fun and we got a extra pair in case one breaks.

That day I was havin' a bad time slidin' my skate on without pinchin' my toes and early on Corrine lost my key, but we finally got ourselves together and was goin' 'round fast as Peggy Fleming and the air on our sweat was coolin' us down while we pretended to fly. We was havin' a good time with our arms all out wide and then Jackie's mama yelled at Joe-Joe same as she did every day at four o'clock to go get the mail. Gettin' the mail was Joe-Joe's only chore and he didn't even do it right and always left the mail box door hangin' down so's his daddy drove into it with their truck every day when he parked, but that's okay 'cause it wasn't my job and it wasn't our truck and Joe-Joe was still little, so mostly I didn't care.

When Joe-Joe run out to get the mail that day me and Corrine stopped flyin' to watch him run out the door and down the circles and crosses and snakes his daddy left when he mowed the yard, and Jackie snuck out her house and up to the side fence and looked through the part in the boards where the knot hole's missin' so's she could see what we was up to. Corrine's head snapped 'round so's she could look at Jackie's eyeball and then she made a few circles 'fore she kicked off her skates real quiet like to sneak up on the side fence and, I swear to Jesus this is true, she jabbed her finger into that hole and liked to pluck Jackie's eye right outta the socket! Jackie screamed at Corrine and Corrine screamed at Jackie and her mama come out the front door and screamed at me so I ran in the house and screamed at my mama. Then it got ugly.

I ain't sure what all happened 'cause about the time Mama went out the front door Corrine snuck in. I left the mamas and all the neighbors that was comin' to look and then I went in and noticed Corrine. She looked sick, like after she ate all the Pepto.

While Jackie's mama was yellin' about raisin' rotten girls and reform school, and my mama was yellin' about peepin' Toms and keepin' mind of your own rotten kids, I took Corrine to have a cool bath. I was tryin' to take Corrine's mind offa all the racket by singin' her How Much is That Doggie in the Window and even managed to get her to sing some with me, and then I wrapped her up in a towel and put her to bed and put on my pajamas and got in with her.

Corrina's just little and still don't have things all figured out. She asked me why was everyone so upset, so I told her.

Chapter 3: Neighbors

I told her that you can't go stick your fingers in little kids' eyes even if they are spyin' on you and pee on your slide. It ain't polite and you got to be nice. She stuck her lip out and twisted her hair and promised to 'pologize, but I think she felt more scared about 'bein caught than about blindin' Jackie.

'Bout that time we heard Joe-Joe's daddy scrape the mailbox door with his truck and start yellin' at the mamas tryin' to figure out what was goin' on in his front yard, and then my daddy come home and didn't even ask but just drug my mama into the house still kickin' and screamin'. I got up to close the door when they got started on each other. Then me and Corrine decided to skip supper if there was one and stay in bed instead of havin' to get up and face that.

In a little while Corrina fell asleep. She was droolin' on the inside of arm when Mama come down the hall and opened our bedroom door but I pretended to be asleep too and after Mama closed the door, I stayed awake for a long time starin' at all the patterns on the ceilin'. I tried not to listen to my mama and daddy and pretty soon they was laughin' at the TV but I still could hear them awful things they all said, just swirlin' 'round my head.

I think sometimes grown-ups just can't be mad and let it go. They got to win or darn near die tryin'. They don't forget about whatever made 'em mad but make it worse by what they say and then can't take back. And they get everyone they know and a few they don't in the middle of the mess instead of just sayin' sorry and tryin' to be nice again.

It was like that with our grown-ups. For a week, Jackie looked like some kinda pirate child that got lost at Trick-or-

Treat. She nearly peed herself again when her mama finally let Corrina get close enough to 'pologize. After that her mama give up tryin' to keep her away from our house where she wanted to play and be friends again.

But our grown-ups never did talk to each other again, not at church, not at the grocery, not when there was parties on our street.

Not even on the day Mama and Daddy stood at the kitchen window and watched them all move away.

My Family Tree
by Corrine

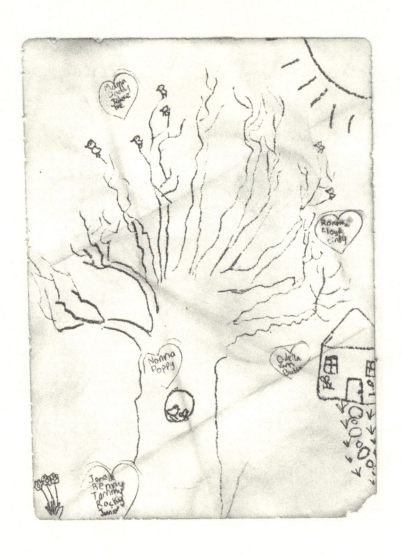

4
Baby Sisters
Corrine

My mama got three baby sisters. She always say Poppy wanted a boy. He never got one. She say he give up after Odella was born. My daddy say that's 'cause havin' four girls scared the life right outta him.

She can make her whole face crazy. When I get sad she cross one eye over to look at her nose. Then she stick her tongue out and make a smile with only half her mouth. When she do that I laugh so hard I can't remember bein' sad. Then I try to do it. But I can't. It makes my eyes jump and wiggle 'til Mama say knock that off or you gonna end up with 'em stuck. She say that's gonna happen to Odella too. You watch. Then Odella straighten her face and look all serious 'til Mama turns 'round. Then we keep goin'.

My daddy picks on Odella which I think is mean. She got a space between her front teeth and Daddy say it's big enough to drop a nickel. One time Odella and me was laughin' so hard her teeth was showin' and she smiled with only half her face so's I'd laugh even more. We was settin' and laughin' and makin' faces and my daddy whispered to Mama to pass a nickel. Mama smacked Daddy on the leg and told him *shush!* the way she tells me when I burp in church or say out loud I gotta pee. Then Uncle Varn told us quit it for Pete's sake. He all the time sayin' Pete's sake this and Pete's sake that. We don't know nobody named Pete.

Odella and Uncle Varn got one baby and that's my cousin Bubba. Bubba's littler'n me. He don't think right yet. He say things that are dumb as a rock. He got the right parts but they don't fit together yet is what my daddy say.

I like Odella's house. She got a big white house with three rooms and a bath. We used to see them all every Sunday for supper after church. Now just sometimes 'cause our new house by Tanya and Brenda Rae's too far from them. Odella be cookin' and workin' in the house or the yard when we do get to go. She wears aprons with flowers and pink house shoes and she always got her hair up in a bun. It's straight as a stick and goes shiny in the sun when she hangs the wash. Sometimes little pieces fly in the wind and I watch 'em like kite strings goin' up high.

Odella don't really say much. She makes good dinners and makes Uncle Varn spoilt and happy. Mama say that's all that matters. And Uncle Varn sure loves her I think. He loves her best 'cause she so quiet and nice. He don't notice her bein' silly. 'Cept that one time my Daddy say about the nickel, he don't ever say nothin'. He likes to walk with his arm 'round her and they all the time put their heads together and whisper. They hug and whisper on the couch when we watch the TV, too. My Mama and Daddy set in the chairs.

We was at Odella's on Jolene's birthday. That Sunday it was Jolene's birthday when she turned nine. Me and Jolene and Bubba was playin' outside on the swings. Then Rocky and Junior and Tammy come over. They's our cousins from Mama's next sister Aunt Jonelle who married Uncle Benny.

We see Aunt Jonelle and Uncle Benny sometimes. Mostly just at Christmas when they let us. Mama and Daddy say they uppity. They got a big house and a big car and all the time new clothes. Aunt Jonelle always wears a dress and gloves and spiky shoes and Benny rubs his belly and burps a lot. They always got new furniture and stuff for their house. Uncle Benny don't like us at their house 'cause he say we don't close the door and let the flies in and put dirty fingers on the couch. He say the sofa. Aunt Jonelle say Chesterfield. Daddy say they should just say couch and get it over with.

Tammy so old she don't play no more so she and Aunt Jonelle just set and talk. But not Rocky and Junior. They find us to play. But them boys is rotten. They just plain mean. I don't like 'em and I don't like to play with 'em. Jolene say ignore 'em but that's hard to do when they get stuck up in my face.

Me and Bubba and Jolene was swingin' but when the grown-ups went inside them boys pushed us offa the swings. Me and Jolene landed safe on our butts so we climbed on the bars but the swing hit Bubba in the backa the head so he went in the house cryin' for Odella. In a while he come sneakin' out with a bag of bread for dough balls.

Uncle Varn taught us how to make dough balls so's he could use 'em for catchin' fish. Now he say he always gotta have a extra bag just for us. If we eat too much we get a stomach ache and later Odella goes nuts lookin' for bread for Uncle Varn's supper. We always throw the bag out and bury the crusts so Odella don't see what we done.

Bubba settled on the back steps and started peelin' the bread. He set the crusts in a pile and then rolled up the bread into little balls. I left them mean boys and went to the steps to roll dough balls too. Every now and then me and Bubba'll stuff so many dough balls in our mouths that we look like squirrels in the yard. Then we laugh and try not to spit 'em at each other or choke to death.

Halfway through the bag Odella come out back. I knowed Odella was upset 'cause she wiped her hands on her apron and looked like she was gonna cry. That Bubba so dumb he tried to stuff the crusts into the bag and give it back to his mama. Odella looked down in the bag tryin' to see what he put in it. Then my mama come on the porch with Aunt Jonelle and yelled for Jolene to hurry up to go to the doctor.

Ain't no doctors work on Sunday. I may be little but I ain't dumb. Ain't no rock settin' on *my* head. So I say to Mama

Chapter 4: Baby Sisters

what doctor works on Sunday? and she say I found one. I say Jolene ain't sick but Mama say she needs shots. I figured I'd need 'em too so I say I gotta get my shoes from the swings. But Mama say no, just Jolene and Rocky and Junior.

That whole time Aunt Jonelle was on the porch pullin' on her gloves and Tammy come behind her with that puckery look on her face. Aunt Jonelle yelled hurry up so Rocky got offa the swings and kicked sand in my face when I run by, so I caught up and spit on his shirt. Mama grabbed me by my ear and started yellin'. I tried to tell her what happened while gettin' on my tippy-toes so's my ear don't come off. Then she set me on the steps with Bubba and say wait here when she went inside. Odella was still tryin' not to cry when she followed Mama inside with everyone else. And then most everyone left for the doctor in Benny's white Cadillac. Just Odella and me and Uncle Varn and Bubba stayed.

Odella finally come out smilin' again. We all helped her with her outside chores and played on the swings and Uncle Varn pushed Odella so high that she laughed for a long time. Uncle Varn give us a bath and clean shorts and put us on the floor in fronta the cooler. We ate our sandwiches and watched TV and laughed and me and Bubba got ice cream. It was dark by the time all them got back from the doctor. Aunt Jonelle and Uncle Benny didn't even come in but dropped everyone in the drive and took off with Tammy and them rotten boys. Then the daddies got to talkin' and drinkin' beer and then it was too late to drive, so we all slept at Odella's big house.

When Mama don't tell me the truth Jolene always does. She tells me so's I don't feel bad 'bout bein' little. Mama say it slow, like I'm too little and gonna cry, but not Jolene. Jolene knows I get it that sometimes things just ain't fair. She tells it to me right. Today Jolene say they didn't go to the doctor yesterday. She say they all went to the movies.

We don't never go to the movies 'cept for the drive-in sometimes where Mama has to work. Then we take our chairs and blankets and sodas and sandwiches. 'Fore the movie me and Jolene play at the playground and I get tired. Sometimes I fall asleep 'fore the movie even starts.

So Jolene told me what Mama told her. Mama say that Aunt Jonelle and Uncle Benny decided that for Jolene's birthday they gonna take her to a inside movie with air conditionin' and they gonna buy supper from the snack bar for everyone. But then they say me and Bubba gotta stay with Odella 'cause we too little and don't behave. I figure they got it all worked out 'fore they even got to Odella's.

But Odella say she want us all to go to the movies 'cause she a baby sister and know what it feels like to be left behind, like you's too little to behave when you ain't. But Aunt Jonelle and Uncle Benny say no. They say all I do is fight with the boys and can't act like a lady. And they say Bubba can't stay still and needs to stay with me so's I don't get upset. That means Odella gotta stay. Jolene say Mama and Daddy wanted to go but Uncle Varn say he ain't goin' if Odella ain't goin', so he stayed with me and Odella and Bubba.

Chapter 4: Baby Sisters

Jolene say they saw a movie with Lizbeth Taylor. Somethin' 'bout a elephant. Jolene say she liked it but it was old. And all the time Aunt Jonelle and Uncle Benny and their rotten boys and Tammy was bein' uppity and flashin' their money 'round. Jolene say it was like they wanted everyone to see how much money they got.

Jolene told me 'bout the movie this mornin' right 'fore Mama took her to help clean some house for a old lady I don't know. I wanted to go too but Mama say no, just Jolene 'cause I'm a pest when there's work. She say I can stay with Odella 'cause Bubba's playin' down the road and the daddies are fixin' cars and she all alone. I got mad that I always got to stay. I tried real hard not to tell on Jolene that I know 'bout the doctor and went to find Odella instead.

Me and Odella did our work just fine. We made the beds and hung Uncle Varn's pants on the line. We even got the water goin' on the flowers but 'fore we turned it on I got down real close so's I could watch the ants. Ants are smart 'cause they can swim outta the water. I like to watch 'em swim. Then Odella say come on and took me to the swings. She pushed me but not too high, like she say Mama used to do for her. She got to tellin' me stories and then she laughed and run into the house.

My swing slowed down and I jumped off to go in after her. 'Fore I could get up the steps to the porch she come back out with a brand new bag of bread. We took it to the grown-up swing under the tree and sat side by each, and then she opened the bag while she rocked us in the swing. She give me a piece and took one out for her and started peelin' her crust. I thought she crazy 'cause she rolled a dough ball and popped it in her mouth and throwed the crust out for the birds. Then I thought I'd be crazy with her and started rollin' my own dough balls.

That's what we did for mosta the mornin'. That and tellin' stories and countin' bees.

We did that for a long time. All the way 'til our big sisters come back for us.

5

Little

Jolene

Today was my birthday. My mama made me a party and all the family come to our new house. But not Tanya and Brenda Rae from next door. Jolene say they not family and we gotta save money.

First my cousin Cindy from my Mama's other sister come all the way from the farm way far away. We don't see them too much 'cause they don't got a good car neither. Today they come early 'cause it's too hot to drive in the day. They told me happy birthday and then Cindy's daddy and my daddy got beers and sat in picnic chairs under the tree while the mamas set out the party.

Then them rotten boy cousins Rocky and Junior come with their sister Tammy who I hate. She say she too old to play and always stay inside with Jolene who acts stupid when Tammy comes 'round. They watch TV and smoke candy cigarettes and talk 'bout boys and clothes and hair. Her rotten brothers stay inside too and watch TV and pick at them which is just fine by me. And Aunt Jonelle who is Mama's next baby sister and Uncle Benny don't never even say hi to no one but just go set outside and all the time sniff like the dog farted at 'em.

Later Mama's babiest sister Odella and Uncle Varn brought Bubba who's dumb as a rock 'cause he's still a baby and don't know how to think. Odella give me a big hug 'fore she hugged all the rest, even the rotten and sniffy ones, and then she came out to set on Uncle Varn's lap. She put her head close to his and laughed and talked for a long time.

Today I got on a dress that looks like the Texas flag. Mama made it. It gots a big white star right over my belly and it's red on one side and blue on the other. Only now the star got some red on it from where I spilled birthday punch when Rocky and Junior hit me from behind while I was drinkin'. Them boys is just rotten. I hate 'em. I don't know why they all had to come at all. They 'bout ruined my whole day.

I got a piñata today that looked like my dress 'fore I spilled the punch. It was a big white star with red and blue streamers and hung up high in the carport. Mama filled it up with bubble gum and licorice and pennies. Then Daddy got the Kodak for my picture of me with my piñata. I wore my

Chapter 5: Little

socks with the lace and my shiny black Sunday shoes even though Mama said black don't go.

Mama made me smile for my picture. I didn't want to 'cause my front tooth is missin' but Daddy took it anyway. Then he laughed and poked my belly and said you got a hole in your head. He thought that was funny but it made me cry. That was after the picture though. I hope the picture comes out so's I can see what I look like all dressed up. Daddy likes to take pictures.

My grandma and grandpa from California sent me a card with five dollars. I ain't *never* had five dollars. It got a picture of Aberham Lincoln on it. I don't know him. I want to spend my five dollars on jacks for me and my sister Jolene to play. We don't have enough jacks. We lost most of 'em when we moved and we don't got a toy box no more. Mama say now we leave 'em out too much and Daddy steps on 'em in the carpet and then he swears and throws 'em out. I'm gonna take care of new ones though. I want those pretty gold and blue and silver ones that come with *two* red balls. I can keep 'em in a bag on the box by my bed so our dog Ginger don't run off tryin' to eat 'em and Daddy don't step on 'em.

After we ate hamburgers Mama and Daddy made me and Jolene be still for a picture with them rotten cousins and Cindy too and then everybody sang me Happy Birthday to You. I got a cake that Mama made like a big white star and it got red hots all in the middle and little blue sprinkles on top. I had to blow out the candles and then Mama and Odella give everybody a piece. Then *finally* I got presents. I had to look at 'em all mornin' on the table with the cake on a plate with a cover to keep the flies off. Then I got to open 'em all.

Then Mama and Daddy let me open their present with shiny red paper and a big white bow. I got me a doll bed for my shoebox house. Last Christmas we got a box from my Sunday shoes and me and Jolene we colored a door and a window with curtains and a rug inside it. Jolene cut out some pictures from a magazine and glued 'em on the walls. It looked just like a fancy apartment room and we made sure to move it too when we come to our new house. Now I got a bed for it. And a doll with no clothes and no hair.

Mama and Daddy don't get me dolls no more. They say I'm too hard on 'em 'cause I lose their clothes and like to play beauty parlor. One time I got me a black crayon and colored my doll's hair so's it looked just like Cleopatra. I drawed blue eyebrows too. I tried to wash the color out my doll's hair but it was all sticky so I cut it off. Mama say that's enough and no more. She don't buy me dolls no more, not even for Jolene, but she still buys us the doll stuff for our shoebox doll house.

I don't care. I got lots of dolls anyway. So what if some of 'em are naked and don't got shoes? My favorite doll only got one. She got one pink shoe but the other one come out in my dog Ginger's poop so I told Daddy throw it out. It's better to have just one shoe than have one shoe and one poop shoe.

After presents I mostly played with Cindy. We got to play leapfrog but you gotta be careful when you play leapfrog with Cindy. Sometimes she falls when she jumps and bumps her face right into your head. One time she was tired and fallin'

Chapter 5: Little

over my back when she shoulda been jumpin'. I had the chickenpox all on my head and she bit it and made it bleed even more. Mama turned the hose on it.

After we played leapfrog we rolled down the hill. In the new backyard we got a hill that's bigger than the one in front. It's hard to mow and sometimes when we play in it we get chigger bites. Daddy was gonna take out the grass and put in a garden like mint plants and stickery roses with another fence. He say the old neighbor Joe-Joe and Jackie's dog give Ginger puppies and he don't want that to happen again. That don't make no sense to me. She grew them puppies. I saw her.

But Mama say you know we ain't got money for no roses and I don't want to have to do weedin' in no damn garden anyway. So we still just got a big hill with grass. Sometimes the grass dies where Ginger pees or where the caliche comes up but then Daddy waters it in good or puts Salts and mixes it up. He worked hard on the lawn for a whole week and said bad words when he went to mow the hill. Mama say you got to mow 'cause everybody's comin' and they ain't seen this place yet, but he said I'm done so we still had grass to roll in. We didn't even mind the chiggers and then we ate more cake and I had a cold bath. I like a cold bath when it's hot and the chiggers get me.

When I come out the bath everybody was gone. Just like that. I asked my mama where'd they all go. She said it's late and we gotta get ready for work tomorrow and looked at Daddy. He made that grunt noise and looked like he was gonna say bad words but instead he went to his room and slammed the door.

Mama jumped off the couch and went in after him, and Jolene looked at me that way she does when she doesn't wanna hear no one. We set in the livin' room and tried to play but all the time Mama was yellin' 'bout I told you there wasn't enough beer for everyone to stay late, and what kinda party is that, anyway.

'Bout dark, Mama come back to the livin' room. She had another present in blue paper with white flowers and curly ribbon. I jumped up but she walked 'round me to go over to Jolene and set on the couch next to her. I think I just froze 'cause I felt like that way you do when you watch a movie, like you don't know what's happenin' but it don't make no sense. Then Mama put the present in Jolene's lap. I looked at my mama with my mouth hangin' open and said it's my birthday, so what's she gettin' a present for. Then Mama screwed up her face like uppity Aunt Jonelle lookin' down her nose and said it's for Jolene for helpin' me make your party today.

I stood there and felt a shake move up from my toes to my head. It started quiet and then started buzzin' inside my head and I thought it would make my eyes bounce 'cause it got so loud. I thought *helpin' with what?* but the words wouldn't come out my mouth. I'm thinkin' to myself she didn't do nothin' all day but set on the couch with my cousin Tammy who I hate and talk 'bout clothes and shoes and hair and stupid stuff. She didn't even move an inch all day and then later she started lookin' down her nose at me and Cindy with her screwed up face and sniffy nose just like the uppity ones.

Mama was all curled up on the couch with her and had her arm around her tellin' her open it. Jolene moved real slow

Chapter 5: Little

like she had clear into next week to open it and show what was inside and I thought it must be a book or somethin' dumb but then you know what? She smiled and said ohhhhh real long and hugged my mama. Her box with the same doll bed as mine slid off her lap and fell on the floor.

I was so mad I liked to wet myself. How could she? How the *heck* could she? How could she give my birthday to Jolene? How come I couldn't have the one thing in the world that was all mine and nobody else's and have it all to myself without anyone takin' it from me? How come Jolene's birthday got to be special goin' to the movies without me and I couldn't even get my very own one and only doll's bed?

Just 'bout that time my Daddy came out with a empty beer can. He took one look at my mama and Jolene huggin' and then looked at me with my face all scrunched up ready to cry and my mouth hangin' open and you know what he did? *He laughed.* He did. For sure he really did. And then he said close your mouth 'fore you swallow flies and kept laughin' some more.

So I let myself cry. It wasn't that I was sad. I was *mad*. I looked way far up at all of them and asked *how could you*? It was my day. Mine! And just like that you took it from me. You give it to Jolene and it ain't even her day or her year even, and you give all the special to her and leave me with nothin'. What is *wrong* with you? Why can't you let me have nothin' ever? Why don't I matter?

Mama came up off the couch and I thought she might hug me and take the doll bed from Jolene but she just grabbed my arm and told me come on. You're tired. You're goin' to bed and get yourself together. You got plenty. We give you a party and toys. You even got money to spend. And then she looked at Daddy and said at least you got that. And all you do is fuss after we all been so good to you.

Jolene was starin' at the floor and kicked her toe at the doll bed and Daddy just went in the kitchen to get another beer. Mama grabbed me harder and drug me to my room and grumbled the whole time she put me in bed and told me you need to grow up and quit bein' so selfish and I tried to tell her. I kept talkin' louder and louder and thinkin' if I just talk loud enough she'll *hear* me but it wasn't no use. I thought this is crazy. I make perfect sense to me. Why's it so hard for Mama to understand? I talk okay. I got words. I make sense. So why don't she see the same thing I see? And why they all gotta laugh at me and be mad at me for feelin' things?

I got more and more mad and slapped my hands beside me on the bed and bent myself all the way over and cried in my knees. Mama finally said *oh, shush*! and turned around and left me there cryin' by myself without even Jolene who I hate in the same room for me to talk to.

So here I am layin' in bed in the almost dark with snot in my hair and thinkin' 'bout what Jolene told me this mornin'. She said to be sure to have some fun while you're little 'cause when you get older birthdays ain't so good. She said that but I don't believe her no more never never never. I hate her and I don't believe a thing she says. They already ain't good.

Chapter 5: Little

If Odella was here and didn't go home I would ask her why today, when my birthday finally came, did they have to go and take it from me? Why do we gotta stay home and not get to go to movies for birthdays like Jolene and Mama do? Why don't baby sisters matter?

6

"This is Most Certainly True"
(Martin Luther, Luther's Catechism)

Jolene

I'm in the third grade. Mama lets me and Corrine walk to school now every day. That's why we moved closer, so Daddy can take the car every day to work at the farm and we can walk. It don't matter. We don't have to cross the street but one time and there's a crossin' lady to help us. She's the principal's wife and all their kids go there, one in every grade and two in third with me. I'm in Mrs. Baumeister's class.

Mrs. Baumeister likes us to say her name like "Bom-my-ster" but when she ain't around, we get to playin' and laughin' and callin' her "Bum-my-ster" and grab our butts when we say the "Bum" part so's everyone knows we're talkin' about our backsides. We got to be careful that she don't see and the principal's kids don't say 'cause otherwise the principal, he paddles us. 'Cept for her name, Mrs. Baumeister's a good teacher.

The school we go to is named St. John's Lutheran School after St. John the Baptist who gave his life and his head on a platter for Jesus. We're not Catholic but Mama, who used to be 'fore she married my daddy, said we may as well be 'cause we do church all the same 'cept we left out the Hail Marys and crossin' ourselves and we do confession out loud instead of in a box. I don't even know what she means by "in a box." I don't know how I'd get in one or why I'd want to, but I don't worry about it too much 'cause we're Lutheran and we don't got to get in one anyway.

I learned the whole church service by the time I was six. My cousin Tammy kept talkin' in my face about how she was special 'cause she was goin' to first communion and got a pretty white dress with all kinds of lace and skirts and little white socks and shiny white shoes, and even a headband with a long lace veil and tiny white flowers, and gloves up to her wrist with little white pearls all over. She said that's how you dress 'cause it's just like gettin' married to Jesus. And she got pictures of herself lookin' like a saint prayin' to God.

It ain't fair. I don't get my first communion until junior high's over but we call it confirmation and have to cover our new Sunday dress with a plain old robe that someone in choir already wears. Sometimes it smells like their old lady perfume. Catholics get to do a whole lot of fancy stuff startin'

Chapter 6: "This is Most Certainly True"

early and Lutherans like me only get to do one thing when we finally get old.

I got so mad I decided to do somethin' she couldn't so I learned the whole service from page five of the red book called The Lutheran Hymnal. It starts with some old kind of song on the organ that don't sound so good and has old words and then we do a bunch of stuff that I had to learn, and I still have to try hard to keep up. Mama says it's easy and she knows it all from bein' a Catholic and we may as well be 'cept for the Marys and the crossin' ourselves and the box. My daddy says we're worse than Catholics anyway and just like cheerleaders at a game the way we always kneel down, stand up, set down, stand up, and pray 'fore we finally get to set down for good, "And all that in the first five minutes!" It makes him growl somethin' crazy. Then Pastor does his big talk and I try not to sleep. Sometimes I play with my dress or yawn out loud and Mama reaches over and pinches my knee and tells me, "Quit!" in a hiss.

On communion day, the service gets about forever longer and we got to chant some extra stuff and kneel two more times, and then they change the creed from the Apostles to the Nicene, and Daddy grumbles every time and says it all means the same anyway so why does he have to learn a new creed just to eat bread and drink wine, and Mama, she pinches his arm and tells Daddy, "Stop that!"

At school, we eat hamburgers every Friday lunch just to make sure we stay Lutheran and no Catholics come into our midst. They're not as good as my mama's but they come with all kinds of good stuff like pickles and lettuce and little packets of mayonnaise and ketchup and mustard. I hate them little packets. They don't open easy and you got to use your teeth and sometimes they squirt in your mouth which is awful and then you don't have any for your lunch. One time Corrine nearly got us sent home 'cause of those packets.

Her teacher is Mrs. Massey and she's the prettiest teacher in school with the nicest clothes. She has dark, dark hair she wears all up on top of her head with curls that go way up. All the teachers walk 'round and watch us at lunch and Mrs. Massey was by our table when Corrine was tryin' to open up her mayonnaise, which is her favorite, but she couldn't open it right and she don't know no better, so she clapped it in her hands real hard. That mayonnaise shot up across the table and landed in a skunk stripe in Mrs. Massey's curls. She turned her head and said a quiet "Ohhhhhhh" that went on for days while she stared at Corrine's hands full of mayonnaise, and I liked to wet my pants. Corrine just sat there with her packet in her hands and mayonnaise on her fingers and then she stuck 'em all in her mouth and started lickin' it up. That child will be the death of me!

Them hamburgers got yucky stuff too like onion and tomato, but kids don't eat it. We get French fries with our hamburgers and that means we got to decide if we want the ketchup on our hamburger or on our fries 'cause we only get one packet. The best thing to do is set next to Nancy 'cause she's allergic to tomatoes and they make her look like she got the measles which makes her embarrassed in front of the

Chapter 6: "This is Most Certainly True"

boys, so if I set next to her I can get her ketchup. Then I got enough for my hamburger *and* my French fries so my Friday lunch is pretty good.

The teachers, they don't like us to leave our tomato on the plate. They walk around and tell us we don't got to eat the onion but we do got to eat the tomato and they watch us 'til we put it on our hamburgers and take a bite, 'cept they don't make Nancy. Then we got to swallow 'cause it ain't polite to spit out food you already chewed and we only get one napkin anyway. After the teachers smile at us we eat some French fries until they go away and then we slip the tomatoes outta our hamburgers and put 'em up under the tables in those little ledges under the edge. If we squish 'em in there just right they won't fall out onto our laps and the teachers are happy 'cause they think we ate 'em.

I used to be real scared to hide my tomato and would slide it down just a little bit so if the teachers ever decided to see where the tomatoes were after we left they wouldn't see one in my place and call me in to the principal to get paddled and call Mama to pick me up. I finally figured out that everyone was doin' the same thing and even the principal's kids and if the principal got me in trouble he'd have to expel the whole third grade. No principal's gonna expel his own kids over a tomato. Now I just hide it where I set.

After lunch on Fridays we go to church 'cause that helps us remember to be Lutherans too. We sing and pray but we never clap our hands 'cause Pastor says that's not a glad sound unto the Lord. One time we got to sing a camp song but some of us started dancin' and Pastor said that was bein' heathens in the House of God so we don't do camp songs no more. Instead we sing a bunch of old songs where they left out all the E's and gave us a bad tune instead, so we gotta sing ugly and squish words together like "heav'n" and "forgiv'n". I have a hard time with those words *every single time*. They hurt my head.

Mostly, I think I like bein' Lutheran and goin' to a Lutheran school with all the other Lutheran kids. I like my teacher. And I like our service on page five of the Lutheran Hymnal. I even like the principal and every one of his kids. But I do wish that God would have taken the tomatoes and left me the E's.

7

The Ring

Jolene

We gotta drive a ways to get to the farm. Daddy says it takes about a hour from our new house next to Tanya and Brenda Rae. He works there all the time now so he drives out on Sunday night and stays in the barn all week. That way he ain't drivin' every day and night and wearin' out the tires on our car gettin' to work and bring back food. He's only workin' there now it's time for cotton pickin'. That means we got more chores at home and we walk a lot.

My Nonna and Poppy live on the farm with Mama's other sister Ronetta and her husband Floyd. They got a girl named Cindy but no other kids. Cindy's kinda scrawny and quiet but I like her just the same. She's always happy and likes to dance 'round in the sunlight comin' through the oaks. Nothin' makes that girl sad, not ever.

Nonna and Poppy lived on the farm since forever. They don't never leave the farm neither. Only time they leave is Christmas and then Uncle Varn has to drive out to get them and take them back 'fore dark 'cause Poppy won't sleep in any bed 'cept his. 'Fore we moved from our old house we came more and always at Easter when it ain't so hot and there ain't so much work, but this year we couldn't 'cause we been movin' all the time now that Daddy can't find regular work. We couldn't come for all summer so Nonna asked us now. She said there's birthday presents she been holdin' onto and it's about time we came and got 'em. Aunt Odella and Uncle Varn are comin' with Bubba, but Aunt Jonelle says she'd rather be dead in Hell than ever go in a outhouse again or break a heel tryin' to get through the garden, so Nonna, she don't even ask her anymore. It's better that way. No one even misses her or Uncle Benny or any of them rotten kids and all their uppity faces.

It's fun goin' to the farm. We always at least stay late 'cause Daddy don't like to drive home in the day when it's hot so we stay over and sleep on the floor and listen to the grown ups laugh. They go forever and finally pull the mattresses out on the porch to sleep out front, and we all trip over each other in the mornin' tryin' to get out to the outhouse. That's the only bad part. They only got one hole.

Nonna's real sweet and I don't even notice that she ain't my real grandma. That was a different lady but she died after Odella was born. I don't know why. She just did. Mama says Nonna showed up on the farm one day and then she just took

Chapter 7: The Ring

over. Mama's face gets stormy when she talks about that whole time so I don't ask. She and Nonna don't talk much, neither.

Nonna's a whole lot younger than Poppy and she don't talk 'less she got somethin' to say. Mama told me she was a picker that was workin' all the farms one after the other and she showed up in front of the gate one day lookin' for work.

Mama was just 16 when my real grandma died. She had to quit school to take care of every one and every thing. She was workin' herself to death in the cotton field and the garden and the barn. I can't even think how she did all that, 'specially with a baby strapped on her front side. So when Nonna come to the gate askin' for work, she just handed Odella straight over and told her to come in so's she could get to makin' some lunch and coffee. Poppy come in later to see Mama settin' at the table with her feet up in his chair and his baby Odella in the arms of a woman he didn't know. Mama didn't even ask Nonna first. She just asked Poppy straight away if he could pay for her to stay a while to help with all the chores and kids. Poppy said that was okay but he didn't wanna pay. He wanted to trade, her work for his name. Nonna said didn't have no place to go and nothin' but the clothes she wore so she figured that'd be fine. And that's how it happened that she got to be my grandma.

Mama don't tell me much of what happened after that 'cept they did a lotta farm work. Jonelle was only 14. She didn't never have to work the farm or help with chores, just went to school and spent her time goin' to weekend dances on the base where she met Benny on a double date with her best friend and his best friend. Benny don't dance now and never did, but he had a car and money and knew how to iron his own shirts, so Jonelle right away married him and went off the farm. They went all over everywhere and Mama said Jonelle come back to visit four months later, showin' off and lookin' like the Queen of England that swallowed a watermelon. Mama was still so mad two days after that she drove the tractor into the creek when she was on her way to the field. And then she couldn't get out. She left it cattywampus up to the axles in water and marched herself over to the neighbor's farm for help. My daddy come straight over to pull the tractor out, only he wasn't my daddy yet. She left the farm right after. But they got married on the porch first.

Mama said she didn't take nothin' when she moved 'cause there was nothin' she wanted to remember from farmin' and hard work and Jonelle. She said all she wanted was her real Mama's pearl ring but Nonna stopped her. She said, "You can't have that now, but you come back in 20 years if you're still married." Poppy didn't say nothin' but let Nonna decide.

* * *

I don't pay no attention to the way things go at the farm. When there's a party Nonna gets things together and it's ready when we get there. But Nonna's gettin' old. She said her back's hurtin' and Poppy's too tired and she needs help with the party, so we come yesterday early.

Nonna and Poppy have to grow mosta their food. They're too old and Uncle Floyd is the only one left to work the fields

Chapter 7: The Ring

so they don't got much cotton to sell. My daddy quit workin' the farm after he got a regular job when I was in first grade. But he had to start back all the time this summer. He works there for eggs and food outta the garden and sometimes when he works on other farms they pay him. And sometimes we get a chicken or part of a hog. Sometimes people give Mama their bean and flour sacks and she makes us shorts. Not many kids got the same shorts so I don't feel ashamed.

* * *

I can't even start to say the things I been seein' today. After we all got up and got the eggs for breakfast and Nonna made a bunch of coffee, Poppy set in his chair on the porch to watch the world go by. Then Daddy and Uncle Floyd went out past the garden and started diggin' a hole.

It was big like you could put a bed in it, and deep too. My daddy jumped down inside of it but Uncle Floyd dropped his shovel and took off toward the road in Poppy's old truck. Corrine and Cindy ran around playin' by the garden and then went to see the neighbor's horse, but I couldn't stop watchin'. I set on the edge of the porch with my legs danglin' thinkin' Daddy was pretty near China and would have to stop diggin' soon, but the hole just got deeper and all's I could see was the top of his head and flyin' dirt. I looked over to see if Poppy noticed but he was pickin' his nails. After a while, he wiped some sweat off his neck and scratched the back of his hand where a fly was.

'Bout the time I thought Daddy'd disappear down the hole forever, Uncle Floyd came back up the drive with two shiny trash cans in the back of the truck. He stopped out front and took 'em out by the garden 'fore he gave Daddy a hand outta the hole, then off they went in the truck to the back of the house where I could hear 'em throwin' somethin' in. They come back a few minutes later with a load of oak my Daddy threw in the hole while Uncle Floyd poured a whole mess of gasoline on it. Then they lit a rag and threw it in 'fore they jumped back from the *whoosh*.

That was enough to make me think they lost their minds. I stood up on the porch and stretched my neck tryin' to get a better look at what they were burnin' in the hole but there was nothin' there, just old wood and termites poppin' and snappin'.

I heard the porch door close behind me and then Nonna was there. She had two glasses of sweet tea, one for her and one for Poppy. They set in their chairs and watched the fire while they pressed those cold, cold glasses on their heads. I moved back and set on the bench between them lookin' from one to the other waitin' for someone to tell me what in the world was goin' on.

My Daddy went 'round back of the house and I didn't see him again but Uncle Floyd went down across the creek and opened the barn door. He pulled a rope from a post by the latch and disappeared for a minute 'fore he came back out with a couple sheep.

I was so excited I jumped up and headed for the steps. "Nonna! Where'd we get sheep?"

"Stay here now." That's all she said.

"No!" I looked over my shoulder to see if she would stop me. "I wanna see 'em!"

Chapter 7: The Ring

"No you don't." She looked at me straight on.

Somethin' in the way she told me made me turn 'round and set myself down on the bench again. I tried not to watch Uncle Floyd walk the sheep 'round back.

I picked at a piece of dirt on my shorts and looked 'round but nothin' happened. I was afraid to move from my spot. I was there for a long time listenin' to the ice in her tea and the wind from the fire.

Nonna finally said, "I got somethin' for you." She reached into her apron pocket and held onto somethin'.

"A long time ago, I came here to help your grandfather with this farm and the girls. You know that. Your real grandma was dead and I was here to help with what was left."

I was tryin' hard to pay attention but I was itchin' to go see them sheep. Nonna was takin' her time to tell her story and it ain't kind to be rude to old people, so I tried not to be mean like Corrine and just get up and say bye. I swallowed and blinked and made myself listen.

"Your real grandma left one pearl ring behind. I never wore it. I saved it for your mama 'cause she was the oldest, but she wanted to leave so bad she'd do anything. I even found her in the cotton trailer one mornin' tryin' to hide so's she could run away when the truck went to the gin. She was done here. She left a week later with your daddy." She started to say somethin' else but Poppy cleared his throat and she stopped.

I knew my eyes were big. Mama taught me long time ago not to let my mouth hang open so I tightened up my teeth and tried to look normal, but I just knew I looked like a big-eyed frog while I waited for the rest of Nonna's story.

Inside, I could hear my mama pullin' the kitchen table across the room. The legs were scrapin' the old floor until it screeched. The screen door out back opened and slammed and I could hear Mama and Daddy and Aunt Ronetta talkin' and pullin' pots and pans down from the old kitchen racks. I didn't know what they were doin' in there but whatever grown ups do is mostly boring anyway. I thought about goin' to the creek to lay myself down in the cool of the water and watch the clouds, but Nonna finally started again.

"She wanted to take that pearl ring, but I wanted it safe and not sold outta desperation. I knew that'd be comin'. So I kept it. And then you came."

She turned her head to look at me. Her eyes didn't even blink when she said, "Big changes comin' up, girl." She pulled her hand outta her apron and stretched it out to me. I saw that pearl ring she was tellin' about when she opened her fingers. My mouth fell open and I didn't even care.

"I won't be seein' you all for a while I think. You keep this safe." And then she took my hand and put the ring on my finger. It was perfect.

Somethin' inside of me knew Mama'd be more than mad and I didn't care. I would never ever open my mouth and say it but I wanted to show her more than anything that I got what she wanted just because *I* am special. I get that special ring even if she hates it. It's mine 'cause I'm Jolene. I don't gotta watch Corrine or clean an old lady's stinky house or be

Chapter 1: Big Red

quiet about what I think or act uppity like cousin Tammy to earn it. I'm *me*, and I wanted to show Mama and the whole world that *I* am special.

'Fore Nonna could stop me I ran to the screen door and threw it open to run into the kitchen.

I still have no idea what I was lookin' at, but I froze. No one saw me standin' there. My daddy was comin' in the back door holdin' a stringy piece of somethin' hangin' by bones and drippin' red on the floor. Aunt Ronetta grabbed it from him 'fore she dropped it in a pot and set it to boil. Then came a long purple piece of somethin' squishy that went into the sink where Mama was workin' the pump handle to get fresh water to wash it off, and then it went into the fry pan with more onions. Pieces of drippy stuff kept comin' in with Daddy and Uncle Floyd until I couldn't stand it. By then Mama and Aunt Ronetta were on all fours with rags and soapy water scrubbin' stuff that looked like chocolate pudding offa the floor.

I felt somethin' move on my back and figured out real quick it was Corrine. I don't know how she got in there or why, but she was reachin' 'round for my hand.

"What is all that?" she whispered to me.

Daddy had set himself down at the kitchen table and was watchin' us while he drank a beer. He looked at the ring on my hand.

"Go ahead," he laughed. "Tell her. Tell her what it is." His eyes never left my hand.

I didn't wanna let him see me cry or be sick, and Corrina didn't need to see no more of this. She's just little. To her sheep are pets you feed and run with in the field. Meat is somethin' you get in paper at the store that makes Mama say, "What the hell?! How much?" It ain't this, and she don't need to see or know any of this yet.

Mama looked over her shoulder at him but kept scrubbin' the floor and never said a word. I took Corrine by the hand and bent over to look her in the eye.

"It's just cookin', silly," I lied, "And they spilled. Let's go outside with Nonna, 'k?" And I held onto her tiny hand while I skipped across the floor and out the screen door to take her away.

Once I got Corrina settled on Nonna's lap, I skipped on down the porch stairs to the back of the barn 'fore I finally threw up my guts under an ol' bent up tree. After it was over I set myself down to wait for my head to settle and braided some long bits of grass. Nonna kept a eye on me while she and Corrina played pattycake on the porch. Daddy and Uncle Floyd put the trash cans in the holes and covered them with hot bits of oak and long wet rags and farm dirt 'fore they joined 'em. Then Cindy come back from the neighbor's horses and helped Mama and Aunt Ronetta bring out beer and sweet tea. And I still waited.

Nobody called for me. I watched the fireflies comin' out and thought about goin' to the porch. 'Fore I did I held my hand up to the sky and looked at my new ring. It glowed by the fallin' light and made me feel loved.

8

Chicken

Corrine

Jolene's hateful.

She know I hate that she got my real grandma's pearl ring and I got a dumb old doll. It ain't fair. She all the time get special stuff just 'cause she got born first and I get stuck with baby things. 'Cept for Christmas when I get a real Barbie, but then she gets one too. I hate her.

Friday night we went to the farm. Daddy been workin' there so he come all the way to get us and took us back, even Ginger. We had to go 'cause Nonna say she want to make us a party but she too old. She say she need help. She say it's pickin' time but everybody gonna stop and help her make a party so we can have our birthdays together. And everybody come on Sunday.

Well almost everybody. Aunt Ronetta and Uncle Floyd was there 'cause they live there with their baby girl who's my cousin Cindy. They say they ain't never gonna leave 'cause Ronetta don't want Nonna and Poppy alone at the farm. But Aunt Jonelle and Uncle Benny and them rotten kids wasn't there 'cause they too uppity to be at a farm. But Odella and Uncle Varn come with my cousin Bubba, who's dumb as a rock. I think he can't help it.

And then there was us and Mama and Daddy. Daddy been workin' there so much now Mama say he might just as well live there. He say he likes it and he brings a whole mess of eggs home every week. I'm so sick of eggs. But I like the chickens. Sometimes they chase me. That nasty one Georgie chases me most and pecks my legs and makes me scream. I like that.

They don't bother Nonna though. They hear her comin' when the screen door slams. She stands on the porch in her dress and her long long apron and holds her bowl of smelly old bits of food. She calls 'em and waits for 'em 'til they all come up front into the garden, runnin' and squawkin' and flappin' their wings that don't fly. Then she throws 'em the scraps and turns her bowl upside down and wipes it out with her apron. She does that every mornin' and every night so's they make us fat brown eggs.

In the back there's the chicken coop that's empty in the day. Nonna lets me pick the eggs but sometimes there's still a hen on 'em and Jolene has to get under 'em 'cause I won't do that. And sometimes there's a snake so Nonna gets her rake and throws it out 'fore we get the eggs. Next to the coop is the wash house with the old machine and the wringer. I hate that wringer. It's 'lectric and you can't stop it if you pinch your

Chapter 8: Chicken

fingers so I don't go in there. It has bugs and big spiders too. That's a nasty place. And way out back is the outhouse. I got nothin' to say 'bout that.

Nonna's not my real grandma. That was a different lady who died after Odella was born. I seen her picture once. She look like Mama. Then she died.

Mama say Nonna showed up one day after that lookin' for work. Then she say I do on the porch with the preacher and Poppy just 'fore she got to work. I think she been workin' there ever since. She don't *never* set down but works the farm chores all day long and into the night, and she don't hardly ever talk.

Nonna took care of Mama and her sisters but Mama helped too 'cause she's the oldest. Now Nonna don't have no kids to help her 'cept Cindy who goes to school in the day. So Nonna and Ronetta do the house and barn and garden chores. Floyd grows the cotton. And Poppy sets on the porch and watches everyone and grumbles all the time 'bout they ain't doin' it right. Sometimes he walks to the barn or out to the creek but Nonna has to help him or he falls down. He's old and bald now so mostly he sets and grumbles.

We help some when we go but mostly I don't, 'specially like now when it's time to pick. When it's pickin' time Daddy and Uncle Floyd and the neighbors come and when they finish then everyone go help at the neighbors' farms. Us kids don't help and Mama say she be damned 'fore she touches another boll in her lifetime, so she helps Ronetta and Nonna with the animals and feedin' everybody and tells us to get out from underfoot. We do. We set on the porch and drink sweet tea and watch the chickens eat the bugs offa the tomato plants. We eat warm watermelon from the patch too and then the cow wanders up and we feed her the green part. We set like that all day sometimes.

'Fore Poppy got old and bald he made us a swimmin' pool. He had a extra one that the cow wasn't drinkin' from no more and it was on its side up by the barn. He told Uncle Floyd roll it down to the flat part by the creek and fill it full of creek water. It's still there and Uncle Floyd fills it when we come and when we leave he pulls the plug to drain it so's it won't be nasty when we get back. Yesterday I didn't want to climb in to pick the dead tree leaves out 'fore he filled it so I laid myself down in the creek instead and watched the thunderheads. Cindy went out back of the fields and climbed up on the fence rails to pet them horses' faces but not me. They too big and snort and stomp their feet and make me scream, and not in a good way like Georgie the chicken. So I laid myself in the creek.

That creek been there on the farm since forever. It runs just in front of the garden and then through a big pipe under the dirt road that goes to the highway. Most times it just trickles a little and there's never enough to swim in. Then I gotta lay flat in it on the rocks and after a minute them rocks get to hurtin' my back and my head which is why Poppy made us a swimmin' pool. But the creek is nice when it's full. It gets deep sometimes so's I can float on my back with my arms all out and cool off. Sometimes when it gets crazy loud at the farm with all the aunts and uncles and cousins I go there alone. I

Chapter 8: Chicken

just float and float with my ears under water so's I can't hear 'em no more. I listen to me breathe. Sometimes I fall asleep.

Yesterday I done fell asleep for so long my face started burnin'. I got myself up and shook my hair 'fore I headed to the house. Jolene was on the porch with Nonna and sayin' somethin' 'bout I gotta show 'em, and I'm thinkin' show 'em what? Jolene run into the house and Nonna just set there starin' out across the garden with her hands all tight in her lap. She always throws her arms open when she see me but she didn't this time. She looked to the gate and didn't move, not her head or eyes or not even her mouth, so I followed Jolene to see what all that fuss was about.

Jolene looked like one of them statues of Jesus at school. She was standin' stark still and stuck in mid-air with one hand out and the other on her mouth and her eyes like a bug. I come up behind her and saw everyone movin' in the kitchen like they had pants on fire, spillin' all red drippy stuff on the floor. I reached for Jolene and tried to feel around her back for her hand, and I said somethin'. I don't know what.

And then she alive again. She turned around and bent in front of me to look me square in the eye so's I couldn't see everyone workin' in the kitchen no more, and then she took me out to Nonna.

She left me with her on the porch and headed off right quick behind the barn. I set there with Nonna in my wet clothes that were mostly dry by then and pretty soon everyone come out the house. They was poppin' beer caps and talkin' and laughin', and Cindy left the fence rails to set on the steps with me. I thought 'bout gettin' my birthday jacks and the red bouncy ball I brung with me in a ButterKrust bread bag but then I figured them jacks'd fall in the cracks of that old porch floor. Instead we played My Mother Went to Sea, Sea, Sea for a long time, even when Jolene finally come back from the barn.

She hit the steps, and then I saw it. Right there. On her hand *right there*. I don't know how I missed it before, but there it was now. A pearl as big as a pea. Settin' in a ring. On her hand. Just like that, like it always lived there, and her walkin' up the steps all uppity like Tammy and Aunt Jonelle.

I stopped in the middle of the Sea, Sea, Sea and whispered quick to Cindy *quit it, now!* like a snake spittin' in the coop. I slapped her hands away and I didn't give a care that she was poutin' like she would trip over her own lip. Then Aunt Ronetta and Uncle Floyd beat tail down the steps to the garden and started pullin' weeds.

Jolene moved across the porch real slow with her nose up in the air, moved Nonna's tea, and set herself on the little bench 'tween Nonna and Poppy's chairs. She folded her hands like she was the Queen of England so's that pearl was there on top for everyone to see. And then she turned her head and stared right at my Mama who stared back but didn't move from my daddy's lap.

This was too good. I kept watchin' like it was the bestest scariest part of a movie to see who was gonna chicken, but they didn't neither one move nor blink nor even *breathe*. My head kept bouncin' from one side to the other and then back again, even when Cindy tried to pick up my hands to play

Sea, Sea, Sea. I slapped 'em away and hissed. Somethin' was goin' on, and I wanted to know what and who and why for. So I watched some more.

Nonna finally stopped it. She stood up and wiped her hands on her apron and said look at Jolene's pearl ring from her grandma 'fore she walked off into the house. Mama turned her head to watch Nonna disappear in the front door. She looked hard at my daddy then moved quick off his lap to follow. No one else moved, so I stayed where I was and watched all the grown ups act like nothin' was up and no one was 'bout to die.

I couldn't hear a thing from the kitchen for the longest time. Once or twice I heard Mama say you shoulda told me first. And one time somethin' hit the floor. But I didn't hear Nonna say nothin'. Finally she come out with her chicken bowl and headed down the steps. Mama followed her like nothin' just happened but only to the porch. She stopped and put the back of her hand on her head to wipe the sweat. Then she shook her head at Daddy and set herself down on his lap again. And that was that.

Nonna called the chickens and threw them scraps up high, all the way to the sky, and watched 'em fall on them pecky chickens. Jolene came up offa her throne and started actin' normal again 'fore she run over to Aunt Ronetta callin' lookie what I got!

And me and Cindy just shook our heads and slapped our way back to the Sea, Sea, Sea.

9
Helen's House of Beauty

Jolene, with help from Corrine

We come home from the farm real late last night. I's so tired I fell asleep in the back of our car even with it bouncin' over the bumps in the road. Corrine was snorin' and I didn't even care. I slept right through it.

When I get that tired Daddy carries me in and lays me on the bed, shoes and all, and just throws a blanket on me. Mosta the time I wake up fine but this mornin' I was scared. The room was all wrong when I opened my eyes. It didn't look like no room I ever knew and the ceilin' had a crack I didn't remember. I thought hard. I knew I wasn't at the farm and I wasn't in my house. Then I remembered that my house ain't my house no more, and now I live here in this old house next to Tanya and Brenda Rae and share a room and a bed with Corrine.

I left Corrine asleep and went in the bathroom to go pee. I wasn't in there five seconds when I heard talkin' through the walls. Mama was doin' mosta the talkin' and gettin' mad too. She would go on and on 'fore Daddy'd say again, "No, listen to me. I'm done. That's it. We're done." Then Mama'd say, "No we're not. I ain't movin' that far. I can still call Odella and Varn."

And then Daddy would talk for days about how tired he was and sick of charity and not a good job left in the whole state, and then Mama would whine like Ginger when she wants to come in and no one'll let her.

I was done peein' but still wanted' to listen' to Mama and Daddy so I kept settin' there. I didn't wanna flush 'cause it makes an awful noise in the wall and I didn't want 'em to know I was listenin'. I stood up real quiet and took a minute to brush my hair. Then when Daddy come out the bedroom and went to the kitchen, I flushed and washed and went to see what else would happen.

I was thinkin' back to how many times I heard this talk before. Mama and Daddy moved us a lot when I was little like Corrine. She don't remember 'cause she was so tiny, but I do. We was changin' houses more than we changed our underwear. Sometimes we all lived in just one little room. Sometimes we stayed at a motel. One time we stayed in a garage but it got too cold. We left some boxes there when we drove off in the night.

Chapter 9: Helen's House of Beauty

Long time ago we even lived with Odella and Uncle Varn for a while, but then Daddy started workin' at the Sunglo Fina so we lived in a apartment and didn't have to move all the time. Just about a year later when I's in first grade he worked at the Santa Rosa Hospital and we bought our house and got Ginger. It was a fine new house and me and Corrine didn't have to share a bed or even the same room, and we had a carport where we could play outside even in the rain. Jackie and Joe-Joe lived next door and our school was just down the road, and we had a pink bicycle we could ride with all the neighbor kids. Daddy helped me learn and took off the trainin' wheels when I asked so's I could chase all them other kids. And Mama went to the Goodwill to get new old things. She bought our cookin' pot with the black handle there and then got so mad at Daddy she beat it on the counter. That's why the bottom's all dented now and it don't set right on the stove. Every time she uses it now she says she'd just as soon keep the pot and get rid of Daddy. I think she means it sometimes.

We lived there for two whole years but then Daddy come home just about Easter time this year and told Mama, "Here we go again." We moved from there just after school was finished and now we live here in this old house where we walk to school. It's next to Tanya and Brenda Rae, and Daddy drives to the farm to go work and bring food. We walk everywhere and clean houses after school 'til Mama goes to work at the snack bar at the drive-in.

Daddy's about done pickin' cotton now it's gettin' colder. He says he don't have no other work. He says we can't live on eggs and old hot dogs from the snack bar all winter long, and I'm thinkin' we must be movin' again. Maybe tonight.

* * *

I still hate Jolene.

She done took all the covers and left me half naked in the bed. I covered my head and tried to breathe my hot air to warm me up and all the time I'm thinkin' she a mean sister. I wish I had a new one.

But then who would I play with when I can't go outside in the dark and get stuck inside? There ain't no one else. I got to suffer with her or be alone. I don't like bein' alone.

I finally got out the bed and went to find her. She was in the bathroom brushin' her hair like she was Tammy with her millionaire. I just yawned and watched her pearl ring that she wears all the time so's she don't lose it somewhere. Halfway through takin' care of myself I asked her what we gonna play today. She say be quiet and don't bother me so's I can listen and then she walked to the kitchen.

I went too. Daddy's at the stove with the grease can and I'm thinkin' I'm gonna have to eat fried eggs again. I am sick sick sick of fried eggs. Daddy say be happy you got food in your belly but I would like to have a peanut butter sandwich more than anything. I looked in the cabinet but the jar is gone. Only crackers.

Mama come out the bedroom with some nickels and dimes in her hand and her big grocery bag. She say she goin' to the grocery to buy us some milk and flour and sausages. Daddy

Chapter 9: Helen's House of Beauty

grunted and shook his head 'fore he turned 'round from the dented pot to go set in his chair. He was lookin at a tore up car magazine when Mama started talkin 'bout well one of us got to do somethin' 'fore we starve to death.

I looked up at Jolene. I guessed we should get out from underfoot again. I took the crackers 'fore we went to our room.

* * *

Me and Corrine made up the bed even though it's so small I can do it myself. She made sure she put her new bear on the pillow 'cause she said it needs to breathe. She says she hates it.

I was settin' on the floor playin' beauty parlor. I knew I had my doll 'cause she's still got hair and both shoes. I made her a beauty parlor apron from a page from Daddy's old magazine. Corrine's doll was bein' the customer but how can you make pretty hair on a bald doll? We just colored her head with a old brown crayon we found in the shoe box doll house.

I heard Mama comin' home and knew we had some food so me and Corrine left everything in the middle of the floor and went to the kitchen. Mama had her shoppin' bag full and was takin' out' all kinds of food. Daddy put his magazine on his lap and was watchin' the pile of food get bigger. He asked her, "Where'd you get all that?"

Mama laughed all happy and turned around to smile at him. "I was at Joseph's check out when a couple of kids come in all loud and that new cashier got distracted. I asked her to give me a dollar for my dimes and she give me a ten. I took it and said, 'Thank you and have you a fine day,' and got outta there as fast as I could. Then I went to Handy Andy and spent it." She turned back to her bag and kept unloadin' groceries on the table. "That'll teach him to pass me over next time I'm lookin' for work."

She got a onion and some sausages and four potatoes. There was flour for sausage gravy and some Pioneer pancake mix and syrup, too. She had a bag of rice and a can of corn and some cereal and milk. There was even some peanut butter for Corrine and two boxes of animal cookies. Last things she pulled out was a diet soda and a bottle of beer.

I watched Mama start makin' breakfast and wondered how we'd ever go to Joseph's again. I was sure they'd figure it out and know it was us, and was hopin' the police wouldn't come to take Mama away. But my stomach was also talkin' so I set on the floor and kept outta the way while she put the groceries away and started cookin'. Pretty soon she set a pan in the middle of the table and told us to come eat. We all sat 'round the table and ate sausage and potatoes and gravy while we laughed and told stories. Even Ginger got some scraps and we didn't have to give her the chicken bones we got from behind Church's. It was pretty fun 'til Daddy put his fork down and said, "That was good, but it don't change nothin'." Then he got up and went back to his chair and his magazine.

I slipped off my chair and grabbed Corrina's hand so's she'd come with me. We put on our Zories that we kept by the kitchen door and went out front to see what everyone was up to. No one was out yet so we set in the yard and picked at the grass. Then I got a idea.

Chapter 9: Helen's House of Beauty

Down the street is a little old car shop. Sometimes it's open and sometimes not. Daddy said it depends on who takes in a car when. He takes ours there sometimes and borrows tools when it ain't workin'. Mr. Albert helps him if no one's waitin' on a car and we watch until we get bored. One time we walked down the street past where we s'posed to go and found a old beauty parlor.

On the front there's big letters sayin' "Helen's House of Beauty" all in black. There's a pink door that's mostly faded and someone took the mail slot so's it just has a big hole like a mouth yawnin'. There's big pieces of wood on either side coverin' up where picture windows used to be, and I think it musta been somethin' to see all the ladies sittin' in a row with their heads under the 'lectric dryers. I told Corrine, "Let's go to Helen's again."

She jumped up and clapped her hands and tried to run in the street but I caught her and reminded her to be careful. And then off we went past Tanya and Brenda Rae's purple mulberry sidewalk and down the street.

On the way Corrina chattered on about stuff I didn't care about or want to think about. I just wanted to get away and not have to listen to anyone argue ever again. I walked slow and listened instead to my Zories slappin' my heels and twisted my pearl ring on my finger without ever takin' my eyes off Corrine. It was a nice walk. Pretty soon we were there.

Mr. Albert had his big gate closed with the chain and the lock so there was no one to talk to first so I stood on the sidewalk in front of Helen's and stared up to the sun at those big letters wonderin' what it musta been like when ladies went there.

* * *

I told Jolene we should change the name. It should be Annette's House of Beautiful Beach Girls because Frankie would like that and he would come visit and sing songs and then they could dance around all the chairs. She smiled and nodded and said mmmmm like that would be fine. That's what she do when she ain't listenin' but don't wanna be mean neither. So I told her again.

She say no. She say there ain't no Annette and no Frankie and no dang beach 'round here.

I told her even I know that. I ain't dumb, but *you gotta pretend!* Then I was off runnin' ahead.

I wanted to see what was *in* there. I wondered is the whole inside pink? Do they got shiny floors and fancy chairs. Do they got them funny sinks you lay your head in and whole walls with mirrors? I stopped lookin' at the letters and tried to look in the hole in the door but there was somethin' blockin' things from the inside. I ran off 'round the side to see if there was a way to look in.

Jolene followed me all the way to the back hollerin' the whole time 'bout slow down 'fore you fall and get hurt. I found a door in the back but the knob wouldn't turn. I got mad and hit the door, and just like that, it popped open.

Now I was in trouble just like Mama but you know what? I didn't even care. I went inside and listened to Jolene standin'

Chapter 9: Helen's House of Beauty

in the doorway whisperin' loud *Get outta there 'fore the police come!* I told her they won't if no one sees us. Just get in here and close the door. So she did.

* * *

I went in and closed the door and could barely see, but there was a window on the side way up high that someone left open and a little bit of light come in that way. I saw dirt and broken bottles that spilled and stained the floor, and a big spider moved across another door to a little bathroom where the toilet was full of awful stuff. I told Corrine', "This place ain't *nobody's* house of beauty. We need to get outta here 'fore I get sick." But she was already goin' to the front where all the ladies used to be.

I didn't wanna follow her. I tried not to follow her. I even told her, "I'm not gonna follow you," but she kept goin' and then I heard her say, "Oh, lookie here, Jolene. It's *pink!* All pink."

Corrine headed for one of the chairs by the hair wash bowl and was goin' to set on it. I stopped her just in time and grabbed an old apron offa the floor. I shook it out and dust floated in the air like itty bitty specks of gold. We laughed and I wiped out the sink and cleaned the chair 'fore she sat down and said, "Wash my hair, Miss Helen," and I did.

We was talkin' and laughin' for a while. I asked if she liked her color and how short did she want her hair and did she want her nails done, too, and the whole time I pretended to scrub my fingers through her little curls while she giggled and talked like a little Mrs. Kennedy. I even turned the water knobs and made watery *shushing* sounds and rinsed the bubbles offa her forehead. She shook her hair and laughed and laughed.

And then one of her curls caught around my finger. I pulled back my hand and felt a tug. Then I watched my pearl ring slip through her hair. I chased after it but it kept fallin', so I tried to plug the sink with my hand 'fore it could go down. It was no use. I watched it fall deep down the drain.

I choked on my own spit. I took a step back and covered my mouth with the back of my wrist and shook my head hard. "Oh, my *Lord*, Corrine!"

She jumped up and stood in front of me, lookin' down the drain, then at me, then back again. "Is it a bug, Jolene?" she whispered.

I couldn't do nothin' but shake. I held up my hand and naked fingers to show her. "It's *gone!* Didn't you hear it? It's gone *down there!* My ring. Grandma's ring. It went down *there!*" I pointed.

And then I fell on the floor.

* * *

I didn't know what to do with Jolene. She fell on the floor. She was settin' up with her eyes open and tears makin' her face wet but no sound was comin' out and she wasn't movin'.

All I can think is I got to help. This my fault 'cause I want to get my hair washed. I got to help her. So I told her set here and don't worry. I'm gonna break that drain and get your ring.

Chapter 9: Helen's House of Beauty

I tried to put my fingers 'round the drain but they too small. Even with both hands I could barely get my hands 'round it. I pulled and pulled but nothin' happened. Then I tried to twist them round parts like at the end of a hose to see if they'd break, but nothin'. I even sat back on my butt and kicked my feet on the pipe but it hurt my feet through my skinny Zories.

Just then Jolene unfroze. She saw me workin' and come awake just in time to grab the dust apron from the floor. She twisted it like a rope and tied it 'round the drain and said help me pull this *hard*, so we did. Nothin' moved.

I was gettin' mad. I looked 'round the room for a stick or somethin' I could hit the pipe with, but there was only old rotten boxes and a toilet plunger. I tried to use it, but it broke in about a million pieces when I hit the pipe.

I told Jolene maybe we can pull the sink off the wall, so we tried. We pushed on it but couldn't get a grip on the dusty floor and kept slidin' away. I tried hittin' it with my side and my shoulder but it hurt too bad and I started to cry Oh, Jolene, what we gonna do?

Then she did the bravest thing I ever did see. She jumped up on the chair and stepped one foot into the sink, then the other, then said hold my hands while she jumped up and down. She musta done that a billion times but still nothin' happened. The last time she tried, she slipped and fell out the sink and landed with her face on the chair. Then she didn't get up.

I knew she was breathin' 'cause her back was movin', and then she let go a sound I ain't *never* heard and said I'm gonna die. I'm just gonna die right here right now.

And then she slithered down outta the chair onto the dirty floor and laid there all curled up like a baby, just starin' and barely breathin'.

I think I believed her. I ain't never scared but I was then. I left her there to go get help.

I ran out the door and 'round the front to see if Mr. Albert showed up yet. There was nothin' and no one there, so I stopped and thought hard.

I finally figured I needed help. I needed Daddy.

* * *

Corrine left and I don't know how long I was there. Couldn't have been that long 'cause I only heard a few cars and the sun was still shinin', but all the dust settled on me. I was startin' to get cold too. I didn't even care.

Then I heard the back door open and Daddy yellin' "Jolene? Jolene, baby girl?" but I couldn't answer. I heard feet movin' fast and then he was bendin' over me and brushin' back my hair from my face. "Jolene?" he asked. "Jolene, can you talk to me?" I just laid there and tried not to die. He kept sayin', "Talk to me, baby girl."

I looked up at him but stayed layin' on the floor. It came to me that he was alone. I sat up fast and looked around him. "Where . . .? Daddy," I whispered, "where's Corrina?" I looked all around the room and started to yell in his face, "Where is she? Where's Corrina gone to? Is she here with you? Where is she, Daddy?" He tried to answer but I kept yellin'. I tried to get up but he pushed me down.

Chapter 9: Helen's House of Beauty

"She's home with Mama, Jolene," he finally said. I was so relieved I started cryin' out loud. He put his arms around me and held me close and rocked me. "Shhhhh, girl. She's home with Mama," he kept sayin'.

He finally pulled away and looked at me. "She told me to come here and bring a hammer 'fore she couldn't talk any more. What the hell happened?"

I cried hard while I choked out the words. I told him we didn't want to be at the house when they were fightin' and came to Helen"s House of Beauty and I was Helen and washin' Corrine's hair and my ring, "My ring! It came offa my finger, Daddy, and it went down the drain, and we tried to get it back but we can't. We can't get it back no more. I lost it!"

Daddy looked over at the sink and then helped me stand. He checked my arms and legs and helped me put my Zories back on and told me to wait for him in the other room, so I sat by the back door.

Then I heard it. There was a giant crash from the sink and Daddy grunted 'fore I heard another. He was swearin' words no one should say ever and I could hear more things breakin' on the floor. Then I heard his boot hit somethin' and things flyin' all over the room. I heard him drop the hammer and I called for him when I thought he fell, but he told me to be still and not move. I could hear him brushin' things 'cross the floor.

When he came to me at the back door he had the hammer but I couldn't see no ring. I looked down at my lap and shook my head 'fore I wiped my tears and whispered, "I'm sorry I lost it, Daddy. I didn't mean to. I never shoulda taken it and I never shoulda been here. It's all my fault."

"Stop that, now," he said. "You're okay. And look." He reached in his pocket and pulled out the ring. I watched him blow on it and rub it across his shirt 'fore he knelt down in front of me. He put it on my finger and closed his big hands around my small one and held us there for a while, his forehead restin' on mine. We didn't say a word.

After a while, Daddy stood up and threw the hammer behind him all the way through to the front door where it crashed with a loud bang. It got stuck in the hole from the missin' mail slot, and he left it there.

I started to get up, but my legs were wobbly. He said I looked like I was gonna fall so he picked me up and carried me all the way home without even breathin' hard. It was just me holdin' on around his neck, my face buried in his shirt, breathin' in the smell of old dirt and sweat and beer, and knowin' I would always be safe.

10 September

Corrine

I got a Godmama. Her name Sookie. Mama say she tried to get four babies but they all fell out. She don't got no babies at all. That's why she end up with me and Jolene.

Sookie got a husband. We call him Papa. He don't talk much. They got a tiny house with just two bedrooms and four dogs and flowers in their yard. We all squished into their house and put our boxes and beds in their shed after our birthdays at the farm when we left from next to Tanya and Brenda Rae. 'Fore we left them girls come over to see how big was our house when it was empty. We hollered in the kitchen to hear our voices bounce while Mama packed the yellow curtains she done made after she painted. She made them curtains the night we scared my cousin Bubba who's dumb as a rock, tellin' stories in our tree house 'bout a skeleton. That was fun.

We been livin' here with Sookie and Papa for a while. Ever since work on the farm run out and Daddy say I can't find no more work. Mama say I'll call Odella and Uncle Varn but Daddy say no. We ain't doin' that. He say call Sookie and Papa instead. That's when we squished in here just 'fore school started up again.

Sookie been in bed since 'fore we moved here. Jolene told me yesterday that Sookie got the cancer. I don't know what that is but it must be bad 'cause Jolene, she done cried. That's why we gotta stay outside after school. Mama makes us stay on the porch and be quiet. Sometimes we float leaves in the dog water bucket but then Mama yells at us quit makin' a mess. Then Sookie calls Mama and say please just all y'all hush.

Yesterday after school Papa come outside with us. Jolene was readin' her book at the edge of the porch so Papa come set on the steps with me. He took me to pick some flowers and then float some petals in the dog bucket and I say let's pretend they're boats. I blowed on my petals and won a race and laughed and then Papa's face got all sad and scrunched up. I was scared bad at how sad Papa was and how he just stared at them petals so I took his hand and brung him to come set on the steps again. He didn't say nothin'. We just held our hands while he stared past Sookie's roses and across the grass to the sky. After we went to bed I heard him tell Mama I gotta get someone to come get Sookie.

Chapter 10: September

This mornin' Uncle Benny and Aunt Jonelle come to get me and Jolene and drop us at the farm where Nonna let us play and feed the chickens. Poppy just set on the porch in his chair like always and watched the neighbor's horses runnin' in the field. Sometimes we stopped playin' to feed the cow or watch a truck go past on the highway. Way late at almost time to close the barn Uncle Benny and Aunt Jonelle come back with those rotten cousins and brung me and Jolene back to Sookie and Papa's.

We heard Mama and Daddy yellin' at each other from where Uncle Benny dropped us by the road. I could hear 'em all the way down the drive the whole time we was walkin' toward the house. Daddy had hold of part of his bed and he was puttin' it in a big truck and I asked Jolene where did we get that truck and she say I don't know. I asked here where is he takin' their bed? And she say we're movin' far away today. I say no we ain't but she say it's true, don't you remember? I told her I don't. You lie. We ain't movin' far away today.

I told Jolene I wanna go ask Sookie, but Jolene say you can't. She ain't here. Someone picked her up today so Mama and Daddy say we gotta go now and can't wait no more. I remember Papa say someone had to come get Sookie. But I sure don't remember no one talkin' 'bout we gotta move far away today.

And I don't remember 'bout havin' to get a truck. We done moved two times already since Maggie died and we ain't never moved in a truck. Uncle Varn just come in the night in Poppy's old truck and we move whatever we can. We leave the rest. We moved that way from our house by Jackie and Joe-Joe. We moved that way from our house by Tanya and Brenda Rae too. Then we come here to Sookie's but now Jolene say Sookie gone and we gotta move far away in a big truck.

Jolene say we need a truck bigger'n Poppy's 'cause this a big move. She say Daddy tired of Texas. She say we gotta go to California and live with Grandma and Grandpa and maybe they gonna get us new shoes. But I don't know them 'cept for when they call on the phone and Mama makes me say hey. I know what they look like 'cause sometimes they send a picture when Mama sends ours, and sometimes they send money in a card for my birthday. One time when we lived by Jackie and Joe-Joe they come and stayed for a whole week and Mama acted like she was from TV, all the time in the kitchen makin' coffee and talkin' nice and makin' us wear dresses and shoes. We had to set inside and talk for a whole week and it made me crazy 'til I almost cried.

Then they went home and we moved next to Tanya and Brenda Rae. Mama hated that new house so she cried and yelled and screamed at Daddy for days. Then she painted the kitchen and made her some yellow curtains with lace. When we come here, she brung the curtains and put 'em in Sookie's room so's they could make her happy. I can see Papa starin' through that window and past them curtains now, watchin' us come down the drive.

* * *

Mama got done yellin' at Daddy and started puttin' boxes in the truck. Jolene say we don't gotta pack nothin'. She say

Chapter 10: September

Mama and Daddy been doin' it all day, but I wonder then why's Mama's curtains still in Sookie's window? Sookie gone. She don't need 'em. But maybe Mama leavin' 'em for when Sookie come back.

Tanya and Brenda Rae and their Mama come to visit and brung some supper after Mama and Daddy got all our beds and boxes in the big truck. We ran and played in Sookie's yard and Mama didn't even yell at us be quiet. Tanya and Brenda Rae say they gonna write us in California. I wonder how long does it take for a letter to get there? I was gonna ask but their mama say they gotta go home 'fore it gets too dark.

When Tanya and Brenda Rae left to go home, Mama and Daddy walked 'em out. Then they come in and Daddy say the truck's ready, and Mama say it's time. Let's go. She say I got the water jugs full so let's just go. That didn't make no sense to me. Why we need water jugs if we leavin' at night? But Jolene say I told you, it's far away and we gotta drive in the days *and* the nights.

We went in the house to pee. Papa was still standin' in the window and I wanted to go say bye but Mama say don't. Just don't. Leave him be and just hurry up and get in the car. I was worried 'bout not sayin' bye.

Mostly I was worried 'bout my new bear. I got him after Mama left my first one when we was movin' here from next to Tanya and Brenda Rae's. It was night when we left there too and I didn't check for him. Later I tried to go to sleep in the back seat of our old car. I couldn't find my bear nowhere, so

I say Mama where is he? She dug in the boxes and say I don't know but don't worry. We'll get you a new one.

I got mad. I yelled *No, let's go back*! But she say we can't. We got to keep drivin'. I hit her arm and screamed at her then *I got to have my bear! He's my bear since I was born and he all alone in that dark house! He don't understand. We can't leave him all alone! How you do that to him?*

She tried to hug me but I hit her hands and threw myself on the seat with my face down in the pillow and cried again and again and again *I hate you!*

I don't want to lose this bear too even though it ain't my first and I hate him, but Jolene say she saw Mama pack him in our old car. She say Mama put our boxes and pillows down on the floor by our seat to make us a bed. I forgot about Papa and went to go see. It's true. My new bear in there with Sookie's blanket from her bed.

* * *

Daddy ain't drivin' the car. He drivin' in the big truck with Ginger and Mama drivin' us behind him. Our car don't ride good and it jiggles when we go 'round corners or over bumps but a while ago Daddy turned us on the highway where it ain't so jiggly. We been drivin' a long time and it's dark. But when he turned I saw Daddy in the mirror of the big truck. He looks like Papa after our boat race yesterday, like Ginger when she done lost her runt.

I'm so scared. We ain't never been in the car this long and there ain't nothin' out here. I hope Daddy ain't lost.

Chapter 10: September

Me and Jolene were talkin' 'fore we got on the highway. Jolene say I will like California. She say we get to live over the garage at the neighbors' by our Grandma and Grandpa's house. She say she guess we ain't gonna live on our own for a while. I asked her if we still gonna see Odella and Uncle Varn. She say no. She say it's too far. We gonna drive for days and days and we can't go back. After that, I couldn't say nothin'. I just been layin' up against her. I been tryin' to sleep but I feel so sad. I hope we're in California when I wake up.

For a while Jolene played with my hair just like Mama does when I can't sleep or when she's tryin' to take away my sad. I been sad before like with Maggie and Ginger's runt. But this is worse. This has scared mixed up in it. Not the kind of scared like the Boogie Man in your closet. Worse. I don't know what's goin' on or where I am. Where is California? And why do we gotta go there anyway?

I'm glad my grandma and grandpa will be waitin' for us. I wouldn't like to be at California with no one knowin' us and bein' all alone. But what else waitin' for us? I know I gotta have a new school and new friends and no aunts and uncles. I won't see Sookie or Papa or my Nonna and Poppy or the farm or even dumb ol' Bubba. I won't see Rocky or Junior neither and that's good. But the rest is bad.

It ain't fair we gotta move far away. Daddy just say we gotta go to California and don't even ask nobody. When I get big and have babies I'm gonna ask 'em 'fore we move. I won't make 'em do stuff just 'cause they're little. I figured that out and I told Jolene too. And I told her I'm goin' to school to be a nurse so's I don't never gotta worry 'bout money. And I'm gettin' new shoes every week and new clothes 'fore church and pack all my lunches in a new box with a Barbie thermos and not use smelly bread bags for my sandwiches but have pretty tin foil. On Sunday I get steak. And I get a TV in color. And I won't be mean and I promise not to be uppity like Tammy or rotten like Rocky and Junior and not dumb like Bubba. I ain't never movin' my babies from their house and I told Jolene that her and her babies and even her husband will live with me and I won't be scared or sad then. That's what I told Jolene.

 She just listened and played with my hair and sang to me but then she fell asleep. Right 'fore she did I felt her cry. She didn't say nothin' 'cause she never does. For once I didn't either. Then she fell asleep and I let her. I just looked outside and watched the highway go by. I can see it 'cause we got a big moon tonight.

 The night 'fore Papa called someone to get Sookie I went to her room to see her. She was all covered and sleepy but she say come up here and see the moon. Then she tell me there's a man that lives in there. She showed him to me outside her window through Mama's yellow curtains. She say all you can see is his eyes and his mouth but he's there alright. When the moon is big he comes to watch all the people down here no matter where they at. He watches what we're doin' kinda like when we watch bugs. I say he must go to sleep sometime but Sookie say no. He's awake at night and sleeps in the day and that way he can watch over us. We watched some more 'til she went to sleep. Then I left her room and the next day Papa

Chapter 10: September

called someone to get her, and I didn't get to say bye to either of 'em 'fore we had to go.

But it's true what Sookie told me 'bout the man in the moon, 'cause every time I look out the window his face is there. I can see him watchin' over us. Really I can.

He's there lookin', watchin' me and Jolene leave Texas.

Corrine C.
September 1968

Acknowledgements

I feel awkward. I've never written one of these before, so I don't know how to proceed. I could fake it and go with chronological order. Or maybe order of importance. Or alphabetical order, or even "most important for last." But, like all things "Lisa," I think I will go with my gut.

Jump in with me.

I first want to reach way back and thank Michael J. O'Brien, my instructor and faculty advisor for the literary magazine production class at Allan Hancock College in Santa Maria, California. He was the first person (besides my husband) who believed in me. He encouraged me to apply for the Pillsbury Foundation Scholarship, and when I confessed that I didn't know what the required portfolio was, he gently smiled and helped me create one so I could apply. He looked past my "green" and taught me the ropes of writing, bringing me into his own neighborhood writing workshop group and helping me navigate the writing business before the days of digital writing and self-publishing.

More than that, he tolerated the ridiculously loud and impossible behavior of the artists and writers who gathered in O14, even when we threw sticky stretchy-man toys across the table to steal each other's work, or (not too often) danced on tables, or watched Lisa burst into a performance of "Sweet Transvestite" in the middle of a writing assignment, or argued and laughed so loudly that we could be heard in the nearest classroom across the parking lot. He, the students he brought together, and the time we shared were all simply magical.

I have had the good fortune to remain in contact with some of those artist friends who have now contributed their efforts to this book. Thanks to Lisa Araujo and Stephen (aka "Stepehen") Davis of Paper Flower Photo in Arroyo Grande, California. Ours was a truly ridiculous and fun reunion/photo shoot; the resulting author's photo is truly appreciated.

I also want to thank O14 friend and classmate Eric Byrne, now of Cheshire Grin Photography in Portland, Oregon. Decades ago, he argued with me (and everyone else) incessantly for editorial changes that were ultimately correct and absolutely necessary, but he was passionate about writing and art. His photograph "Alice, framed and aged by Terrie England to the beautiful work at the end of this book, is the only photo I ever considered.

The art you see in the book is the result of the work of three different artists. Book Coach Emily's daughter, Gidget Thursday McCorkle, perfectly captured Corrine's family tree in a way no adult could produce. My thanks, again, to friend Terrie England for aging it beautifully.

And then there are the small drawings in each chapter, the result of the musings and talents of my sister Debra

Armstrong. When I couldn't find an artist who understood the vignettes I was trying to capture, I reached out to her for help. Luckily, she reached back and exactly portrayed what I envisioned. Thanks, Sis.

I also need to thank my book coaches, starting with Emily Minster McCorkle of Boerne/Comfort, Texas. Emily and I met 20 years ago before she was a McCorkle, when we were both in the English teacher training cohort at Region XIII in Austin, Texas, circa 2006. We never worked in the same schools, but we stayed in touch through district training and social media, both of us surviving the politics of teaching with giant helpings of sarcasm. I came to know her as a voracious reader with an unmatched intellect for analyzing literature, so when I needed a book coach for the writing phase, there was no question who I would ask. Even with a full-time (plus) life as a wife, mother, homesteader, home-school teacher, and the sole tutor at Miss Emily's School of Education and Enlightenment, she readily agreed and eked out time for coaching and emotional support during this project.

Most people don't have a clue how hard a job that is. Emily was tenacious in seeking revisions that, in the end, really mattered, sometimes leaving us both muttering and exhausted, but plodding on for the sake of the art. She gently chastised me when I lost a character's voice or said I'd had enough, then quietly praised me when my writing was so perfect that it made her cry. She spent countless hours reading and re-reading and commenting, and then more hours in Zoom conferencing, going over the work word by word, line by line, until she could absolutely *breathe* every character I wrote.

She also listened to me beg for a deadline extension because grades were due, and all the tomatoes came on at once and needed to be canned, and I forgot about lesson plans, but the trees needed pruning. Then she would say yes and ask for her own extension because she needed to work in a tutoring session, or a riding lesson, or work on getting the snakes out of the chicken coop, or go to Florida to hand-shear sheep, or maybe take a much-needed anniversary vacation. For months, our real lives melded and intertwined in this magical imaginary world surrounding Corrine and Jolene. I thank you, Miss Emily, for all of it.

I would be remiss if I did not also acknowledge the help of author and friend Daniel Gatlin and his wife, Stephanie, my book coach during the production phase of *Mulberries*. Daniel and I were teaching colleagues during my first years returning to California. I discovered that he was writing his first book, *Maiden to None*, during an informal workshop group we created during Covid. After his book was released, his success inspired me to try, to dig the box of stories out of the closet, and to not leave this world wishing I had published *Mulberry Seeds*. Once I decided to do so, his wife Stephanie stepped in and agreed to help as a post-writing book coach. She said it wasn't a big deal, but I know how many hours of frustration and crying she saved me. For me, it really was a big deal.

And then there's Valerie Lowry Edwon. She was my big sister and the inspiration for the character of Jolene. Lots of her

Acknowledgements

personality comes out in Jolene's traits, but what mostly shows in Jolene is the way Valerie always, no matter what, fiercely loved and protected me. I will always regret that I didn't take the time for that last phone call with her. I'll tell that to her beautiful face someday, but for now, I'll tell the world that I thank her for all she gave me. And for never forgetting me while I was figuring things out.

I can't finish without thanking my number one fan, Steve Smith. He saw me years ago on the same day we started work at an oilfield service company, and we both instantly hated and avoided each other. Things changed a few weeks later when it was 110 degrees by noon, and I discovered he was single and living in an apartment with a pool just a few blocks away from my best friend. A casual "Gee, do you think we could use your pool?" led to an invitation. Forty-six years later, we still drive each other nuts.

He somehow keeps things grounded while I lead an unconventional life. I starve for the feel of deep experiences, and he thrives on quiet and solitude. We work together, though, because he never holds me back. Instead, he says, "You go, and I'll be here when you get done." So I move into dorms when I'm 40, I move to Texas to be near aging parents while trying to figure out what I want to be when I grow up, I go on vacations just to see what's there, I make colossal mistakes while I do what I call living, and he is patient with my explorations. When I fall hard, he picks me up, dusts me off, and reminds me that I walked the Louvre in heels.

Then he braces for my next insane idea. When it comes, as it inevitably does, he cheers me on. He's the guy who let me take over the office (and his wallet) while I finished a book I started twenty years before. The one who traveled with me to Wales so I could go ziplining for my 64th birthday and see Stonehenge before I die. The one who fixes things before I know they're a mess, even me.

My dearest Steven, thank you for all you've given to this project, and for always having faith in me.

About the Author

Lisa-Behrens Smith has always been a writer. After spending her high school years in Bakersfield, California, studying journalism and creative writing, she married, had children, and pursued a paralegal career until a change in her husband's employment took her far from her expected life.

Resettled in Santa Maria, California, she left the legal field to raise her children, pursued a degree at the local community college, and accidentally began writing again. On graduation, she was awarded the Santa Barbara Foundation's Edith Pillsbury Creative Writing Scholarship and was then accepted as a Regents Scholar into the literature program at the College of Creative Studies at the University of California Santa Barbara.

At the age of 40, and with encouragement from her husband, she moved into the student dorms over an hour away. During the next few years, she studied, wrote, and won awards at the Santa Barbara Writers Conference before the sudden death of her sister retired her stories to a box in the back of her closet.

Twenty years later, the box has finally been opened and her pen uncapped.

Lisa-Behrens Smith now teaches junior high English in Bakersfield, California. She lives with her husband of 46 years, their difficult cat, and a mind filled with words.

Made in the USA
Las Vegas, NV
21 April 2025